Theodore

The

odore

◁▷ A NOVEL BY ▷

David Melton

INDEPENDENCE PRESS
Drawer HH, Independence, Missouri 64055

COPYRIGHT © 1977 David Melton

All rights in this book are reserved. No part of the text may be reproduced in any form without written permission of the publishers, except brief quotations used in connection with reviews in magazines or newspapers.

ISBN 0-8309-0196-5

Book design by David Melton

Printed in the United States of America

Second Printing—1978

Other books by David Melton

Author:
  TODD
  WHEN CHILDREN NEED HELP
  BURN THE SCHOOLS—SAVE THE CHILDREN
  CHILDREN OF DREAMS—CHILDREN OF HOPE
  A BOY CALLED HOPELESS

Author and Illustrator:
  I'LL SHOW YOU THE MORNING SUN
  JUDY—A REMEMBRANCE
  THIS MAN, JESUS
  AND GOD CREATED. . .
  HOW TO HELP YOUR PRESCHOOLER
    LEARN MORE, FASTER, AND BETTER

Illustrator:
  WHAT TO DO ABOUT YOUR BRAIN-INJURED CHILD
            by Glenn Doman
  HOW TO BE YOUR OWN ASTROLOGER
            by Sybil Leek
  GOOD-BYE MOMMY
               by Bruce King Doman
  IMAGES OF GREATNESS

Designer:
  HAPPY BIRTHDAY, AMERICA!

I know it's folly to complain
Of whatsoever the Fates decree;
Yet were not wishes all in vain,
I tell you what my wish would be:
I'd wish to be a boy again,
Back with the friends I used to know;
For I was, oh! so happy then—
But that was very long ago!

From "Long Ago"
By Eugene Field

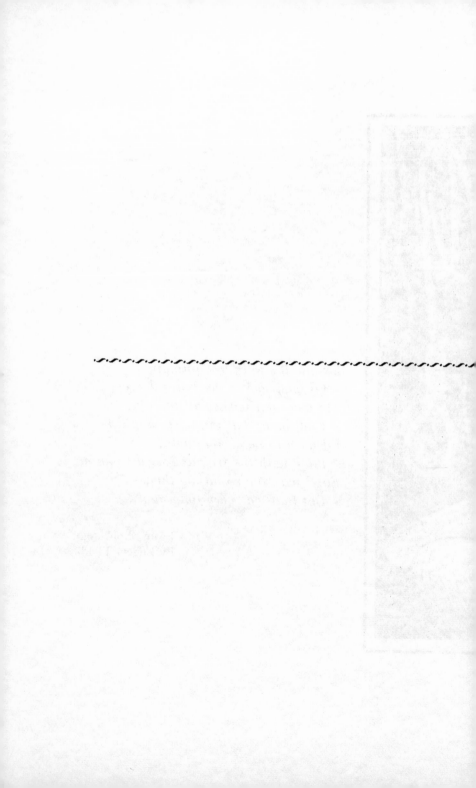

August 13, 1953

Throughout the night, shadowed figures had invaded the old woman's dreams. In the early morning, Etta Pearson awakened and left her bed, but the threatening forms did not remain in her sleep. They pressed her conscious mind, prodding her to remember what they had told her.

Her body moved routinely as she dressed. She scrubbed her face, briskly, and ran the comb through her hair. After straightening the bedding and replacing the quilted cover, she walked into the kitchen to prepare her breakfast, still trying to recall whatever it was she needed to remember.

Soon, the bacon hissed and sputtered to crispness. Shells were cracked precisely against the rim of the cast iron skillet. Eggs were gently released into the heated grease, their yolks standing, round and firm, while the whites became opaque. Together, they resembled two surprised eyes, reminding Etta of the funny singer who sang, "If you knew Suzie like I know Suzie." What was his name? She couldn't recall. Albert somebody. Jewish man. Nice though. No, it wasn't Albert. Edward. . . Eddie. . . Eddie something or the other.

"Silly fool," she told herself. "What difference does it make?" But she thought again. Eddie Jordan. No, Jordan sounds more like a Christian name. His name had something to do with a Jewish preacher. Eddie Rabbi. No, that isn't right. "Oh, Etta, stop it!" she finally demanded.

She carried her plate to the table, placed it next to a bowl of steaming oatmeal and sat down. Folding her hands before her, she prayed aloud, "Our heavenly Father, thank you for the food set before me. May it nourish my body as your love nourishes my soul. Amen."

Etta unfolded her napkin and spread it open across her lap. She showered the oatmeal with heaping teaspoons of sugar, then filled the remainder of the bowl with heavy cream. Breakfast was a ritual that Etta enjoyed. She stubbornly refused to slight or rush her "morning starter" as she called it. She prepared large, farmhand portions, but their generous size never concerned her. She didn't approve of the appearance of skinny people—to her, they always looked sickly and frail.

Although she realized that she must, eventually,

confront the images from her dreams, she refused to allow that prospect to interfere with her morning meal. Instead, she tried to think of the Jewish singer's name, and wondered whether or not she should finally dig out her rosebushes come fall.

"Wish I could find someone to give them to... someone who would take proper care of them," she thought. "Someone who lives far away so I wouldn't know if they were treating my flowers right or slowly starving them to death."

She sat alone. She ate alone. Only the whistle-shrill chirps of the yellow canary she called "Petey" kept her company.

Her mornings hadn't always been met in silence. In years past, they had been filled with voices of people stirring about, laughing, and talking of plans for the day. She had been accustomed to cooking for many plates. At only twelve years of age, she had been responsible for preparing meals for thirty farm-hands at harvesttime.

Ah, yes, *then* her mornings had been full of bustling activity. The sounds of her sisters, Dorothy and Agnes, rushing outside to the handle pump, washing their faces in icy water from the spring-fed well, were expected routine. So were nudges of elbows and disgruntled remarks.

"Etta, Dottie pushed me!"

"I didn't mean to."

"You did too! You never wait your turn."

"It was an accident!"

"Wasn't either!"

"Yes it was!"

"Stop it, both of you! You'll wake Mama."

And, of course, there was Theodore....

Theodore...eagerly darting between his sisters, grabbing the towel, and shaking the water from his head.

"If you don't stop that, I'll tell!"

"Etta, Teddy's getting us all wet again!"

"Theodore!"

"And he didn't use soap."

"Tattletale!"

"Stop that right now or I'll come out there and give all three of you what for!"

Theodore...pulling rocks out of his pockets, and pieces of string, and marbles, and sometimes a recently found frog.

"Etta! He's got another one!"

"Shhh!"

"Get that ugly thing out of here!"

"Looks just like you!"

"Theodore, come in here this instant!"

"Yes, ma'am."

Theodore...running his fingers through his hair, trying in vain to press down a stubborn cowlick. He was a boy with quick smiles and unbounded ideas for mischief...and too many freckles to count.

"So you have another frog."

"Yes, ma'am."

"And where, might I ask, did you get it?"

"Under the porch."

"And I suppose you expect me to believe that it

hopped all the way from the creek to the house?"

"Well, it might have had a little help."

"Put that critter outside and wash your hands again—this time with soap!"

Theodore. . . .

Etta couldn't remember having ever thought of Dorothy and Agnes and Theodore as her sisters and brother. She considered them as responsibilities. Dorothy was eight years her junior. Theodore was three years younger than Dorothy, and Agnes was the baby of the family being two years younger than her brother.

There had been other brothers and sisters in the years between—the markers in the cemetery beyond the church offered sad reminders of the number. There were six small stones; each registered a single date, signifying both birth and death.

On Sundays, before church services, their mother often placed flowers at the tiny graves. And although she never mentioned them during the week, Etta knew the loss of the babies was constantly in her mother's thoughts—so much so, in fact, that Mrs. Morrison often withdrew from reality.

Etta could still see her father coming from the barn, walking toward the house. And she could hear their collie, Zeke, barking at the crows as they swooped down to pilfer the scattered corn which was meant for the chickens.

Years later, there were mornings in her own kitchen with her children. They chattered and laughed and teased each other in much the same ways her sisters and brother had done. Then, all at once. . . it was over. Her youngsters grew up and married. They had homes of their own and children of their own. They were gone. Now, there was only her canary to break the silence.

Just the Sunday before, on the front steps of the College Street Baptist Church, Etta had told Fran Willoughby that although she had lived seventy-two years, she could count only five meaningful decades in her life.

"By the time I was ten, my childhood was gone," she had said. "I had to quit school because my mother's health was poor. I was expected to take on the responsibilities of running the house, taking care of my brother and sisters, and working in the fields with Papa. In my twenties, I was married and had children. In my thirties, I saw my children become adults. In my forties, I saw them marry. When I was fifty, Frank died and I was a widow. Not much of any real consequence has happened since then. . . except I keep getting older."

"Etta Pearson!" she abruptly interrupted herself. "Stop that this instant! Nothing good comes from self-pity!"

With her hand moving a piece of toast in a circular motion, Etta soaked up the remaining yellow of the egg that had escaped her fork. Only after she had finished eating her food would she at last fill her cup with coffee. She respected coffee too much to use it for washing down a meal. Her coffee was made strong, and she drank it while it was piping hot, savoring both its aroma and flavor.

The reverberating chimes sounded from the hand-carved wall clock. Although she was well aware of the time, she mentally counted each stroke. . . one, two, three, four, five. Then, she automatically checked her wristwatch to see if it agreed. It did.

Etta refilled her cup with steaming coffee, walked to the kitchen window, and looked outside. The sunlight streamed across the yard, glistening as it reflected on the heavy dew.

This morning, everything seemed to remind her of the night's troubled dream. The lazy shadows stretching over the lawn duplicated the murky forms that had moved in her sleep. Not being able to clearly recall the shadowy images annoyed her.

The yellow canary fluttered from one perch to the other, flapping his wings against the thin spokes of the wire cage, chirping sudden, shrill sounds.

"Pretty bird," Etta raised her voice in a high falsetto, "Petey's a pretty bird. Yes, you are—you're a pretty bird."

She squeezed her finger between the spokes and the canary pecked at it.

"Give me a kiss," she coaxed. "What a pretty bird."

When her coffee cup was empty, she gathered the dishes and set them in a basin of hot, soapy water. After she wiped the kitchen table clean, she spread the checkered cloth across the top, and placed the butter tray next to the relish rack. Finally, Etta unfolded a white covering and spread it over the tabletop. Held at a peak in the center by the three-tiered relish stand, the cloth somewhat resembled a white shroud. Etta washed the dishes, rinsed them with boiling water, and dried each piece with vigorous, polishing motions.

The white frame house on the corner of Walnut and La Fontaine in the southern Missouri city of Springfield had been her home for the last twenty years. She had bought it with the money from her husband's insurance and the sale of their farm. In the following years, what savings she and her husband had accumulated had dwindled. Now, her only income was a meager union pension and, during the summer months, she sold vegetables she grew in her garden. Now and then, there would be a five-dollar bill folded between pages of letters from her daughters—Marguerite in Minneapolis or Pauline in Seattle. Occasionally, her only son, Robert, would hand her a dollar or two and tell her not to spend it all in one place. But she never spent any money that Robert gave her. She kept it in the top dresser drawer for she knew he would soon return in need of a loan.

Etta walked outside and stood in the backyard. Resting her hands in the curve of her well-padded back, she tilted her head upward and smelled the air. Instinctively, her head turned as an animal's might to survey and analyze its territory. She observed the suspended leaves on the slowly moving tree branches. Her eyes followed the straight, even rows of carrots, cabbages, and tomatoes. Each plant was equally spaced in the planned order that Etta's nature demanded.

The old woman turned sharply as a stray, spotted mongrel pup pranced into her yard.

"Get!" she scolded hoarsely.

The pup scooted backwards and stopped at the sidewalk. There, he sat down and, turning his head from one side to the other, opened his mouth in a quizzical, smiling expression.

"Go on, get out of here!" she said crossly. "I saw what you did on my tomatoes yesterday. Shame on you! Sneaking around when you thought I wasn't looking—defiling my tomatoes like that! Shame!" she repeated. "Bad dog!"

She carried the hoe and shovel from the garage. Hers were not the flimsy, colorfully painted implements sold in supermarkets. They were man-sized tools meant to dig deep into the dirt, not merely to chop at it. As she moved across the yard the dog watched her, waiting, but not daring to step onto the grass. Reaching the other side of the yard, Etta leaned the hoe against the fence, and then turned back to look at the pup.

"You might as well go on," she told him. "I'm not going to feed you anymore, you little sneak!"

She carried the shovel to the back corner of the yard where a load of cow manure had recently been delivered. She dutifully began to carry shovelfuls to her rose beds. Her neighbors had often complained about the odor that reeked from that corner, but their grievances had fallen upon deaf ears. Etta continued to order manure and spread it into the patches of black soil by the fence where her roses flourished. After applying several shovel loads to the area, she looked back to see if the dog was still there. He was.

"All right," she finally said. "If you're sorry for what you did and if you promise to stay away from my garden, I'll give you the scraps I just happened to save."

Etta brought a tin pan of bread crusts and bones from the back porch and placed it in front of the puppy's excited face.

"Not much there, I'm afraid," she apologized as she watched him eat. "I don't leave much waste. You should find you a family up the street with lots of leftovers instead of coming here pestering me."

The pup soon finished his breakfast, and after the old woman patted the top of his head, he set out across the street to continue his usual rounds.

The hoe cut deep into the black dirt and deftly turned the soil. Again, the dream of the night before came back to her in fleeting recollections. There had been a distant voice calling her from the darkness, she remembered. But fences had separated her from the caller. From past experience, Etta had become wise enough to listen to her dreams and analyze them for meaning and guidance. This dream was a warning. She felt it. She knew it. Although she tried to retrace the details, they eluded her.

"Mrs. Pearson," a voice called from the next yard. Her neighbor, Hattie Connell, a tall, raw-boned woman, walked to the fence. "Mrs. Pearson," Hattie repeated, and reaching across, she touched Etta's shoulder.

"Oh!" Etta suddenly jerked and stood up straight. "Hattie," she exclaimed, "you startled me. You shouldn't scare people like that!"

"I'm sorry," Hattie said. "How are you feeling this morning, Mrs. Pearson?"

Etta raised her hand to push back the white wisp of hair that had fallen across her forehead. "Oh, I'm no good, Hattie. "I'm no good at all. I hardly slept last night—dreamed all night...crazy dreams!"

"Is your arthritis bothering you again?"

"Look at my ankles," Etta pointed, "all puffed up like balloons. It's nothing but age, Hattie, nothing but age."

"Your roses are lovely," her neighbor smiled. Bending down, Hattie pretended to sniff the fragrance, but the odor of fresh manure was almost overwhelming.

"Roses," Etta thought aloud, "yes, they're beautiful, but they require too much work. This is the last year for them here. Come fall, I'm going to get rid of them."

"You said the same thing last year."

"But I mean it this time," Etta said, flatly. "Are you about to leave for school, Hattie?"

"Yes, in a few minutes," she answered, looking up at the yellow sun suspended alone in the clear, blue sky. "Looks like it's going to be a hot one again today."

"Doesn't seem right," Etta observed. "You *teach*

school all winter and *go* to school all summer. Don't you ever get tired of being in classrooms?"

Hattie considered the thought. "It keeps me busy," she reasoned aloud. "Since Mother died, I have more time than I know what to do with."

"Why didn't you ever get married?" Etta asked abruptly.

Hattie's laugh was forced. "You must have noticed, Mrs. Pearson, I am no raving beauty."

"No, you're not," Etta agreed, seriously, "but I've seen homelier women marry more times than I can count. And I've even seen downright ugly women take husbands away from good-looking wives. I certainly never thought their kind were women of high morals, if you know what I mean." Etta's face broadened into a wrinkled smile and her eyes sparkled for she thought her statement had been bold, perhaps even risque.

Both of them laughed.

Suddenly, Etta raised her hand with the index finger extended. "Cantor," she said.

"Cantor," she repeated. "Eddie Cantor. He's the one who used to sing, 'If you knew Suzie like I know Suzie.' "

"Why, yes, I think he was," Hattie replied, wondering what had prompted the sudden announcement.

"Been trying to think of his name all morning, ever since I cooked my eggs," Etta told her. "I can't think of anything anymore. Names... they're the hardest to remember. The more recent ones are worse. If I weren't a Christian, I'd bet you that I could tell you the name of everyone in the school I attended sixty years ago—and I'd win too. But if you ask me the name of someone I met yesterday I'd be up the creek without a paddle for an answer."

Hattie looked at her wristwatch and pointed to it to attract Etta's attention. "I'd better be going. Don't you stay out working too long. It's going to be a scorcher."

"Better take your umbrella," Etta advised. "It'll be raining by the time you start home."

Hattie nodded her head at Etta, and walked toward her house. As she ascended the steps to her back porch, she paused to look at the sky as if to confirm her neighbor's weather forecast. From horizon to horizon, there wasn't a cloud. "Not likely to rain," Hattie thought, but she decided to take her umbrella anyway.

"If the weatherman had my swollen ankles, he wouldn't make such a fool out of himself," Etta said to herself as she returned to hoeing the rose beds.

Soon Hattie, with an umbrella tucked under her arm, stepped outside, stopping only long enough to shake the doorknob to reassure herself that it was securely locked.

Etta glanced up to see Hattie hold her umbrella aloft to show she had heeded the advice. Etta nodded and waved. She was pleased that Hattie had also taken her raincoat.

Etta heard the engine start, and saw the Volkswagen move out of the driveway.

Moments later the sound of Hattie's car horn caught her attention. She was surpised to see the car pull back into the drive. As soon as it stopped

Hattie got out, and began running, stiff-legged, across the grass. She waved her hands in the air and pointed toward the front of Etta's house.

"Mrs. Pearson," she said anxiously, "there's a young man at your front door."

"Who could that be?" Etta wondered.

Hattie hurried through the gate to meet Etta and accompany her around the house. Breathing heavily, Hattie said, "I think he's from Western Union. It's hard to tell anymore. The boys used to wear those brown uniforms and ride bicycles. Now they wear street clothes and look just like everyone else. But he does have an envelope in his hand and I think it's a telegram."

"Here I am," Etta called to the boy.

The young man stood on the porch and waited for the women to come up the steps.

"Western Union," he said, dully. "Are you Mrs. Frank Pearson?"

"Yes," she nodded.

He held out a pad and pencil. "Sign here," he instructed.

Etta rested the pad against the banister and carefully wrote her name. The boy exchanged the telegram for the pad, leaning back against the porch column to wait.

Etta broke the seal of the envelope and unfolded the yellow sheet. Her face tightened.

"Is it bad news?" Hattie questioned.

Etta breathed a heavy sigh. "I don't know," she said. "My glasses are all fogged up."

She sat down in the rocker, reached into her apron pocket, and pulled out a handkerchief. She removed the wire-framed glasses from her face. As Etta cleaned each lens, Hattie nervously edged closer.

Then Etta looped the wire frames back over her ears, carefully adjusting the metal bridge into position on her nose. She smoothed the yellow paper across the flat of her thigh, then held it up with both hands. As her eyes followed the printed lines, her fingers tightened against the paper. She looked up and stared straight ahead, not focusing on either the front yard or the passing cars. Flickering images of the dream appeared before her.

She saw herself standing alone on the windswept Kansas plains. A distant voice called her name.

Hattie interrupted her thoughts. "What is it, Mrs. Pearson?"

Etta offered no answer. Instead, she once again looked down and reread the message.

"It's my brother," her voice trembled. "He's terrible sick. 'Critical condition,' it says."

The boy shifted his shoulder against the post. "Do you want to send a reply?" he asked, indifferently.

Etta looked up at Hattie. "I guess I should."

The boy held out the pad but made no offer to move toward them. So Hattie walked over and, giving the boy a look of disgust, took the pad.

"Would you like me to write it for you?" she asked, sitting down in the porch chair next to Etta.

"If you don't mind," Etta replied, taking a deep breath. "Now let me see," she said, trying to gather

her thoughts. "August 13, 1953...Dear Dr. Watts:" she spoke, carefully, squinting her eyes, thinking about the next words. "Thank you very much for the telegram you sent me in regards to the critical condition of my brother, Theodore Morrison. Of course, I am concerned about his condition, and I will travel to Osawatomie as soon as I can make arrangements."

She turned to Hattie. "Does that sound all right?"

"They charge by the word. I think we could shorten it."

"All right," Etta agreed.

Hattie turned the page and started again on the second sheet. When she finished, she read the revision to Etta. "Received message regarding condition of brother—stop—will be there soon as possible—stop—signed, Mrs. Frank Pearson."

Etta was concerned. "You don't think that's too abrupt?"

"Telegrams usually are short and to the point." Hattie smiled reassuringly.

"All right," Etta said turning to the boy. "How much will that cost?"

"It's a minimum. That'll be a dollar twenty-five," he answered dully.

Etta got up from the rocker. "I'll get the money," she said.

While her neighbor was inside the house, Hattie reread the message. When Etta returned, she counted the money she held in her hand—"fifty, seventy-five, one dollar, ten, fifteen, twenty, twenty-five." Then she recounted it as she placed each coin in the boy's hand. She read the message Hattie handed her once more, then gave it to the boy. He stood, waiting silently, looking at the two women.

"What are you waiting for, young man?" Etta wanted to know.

"I usually get a tip!" the boy announced.

Etta's look was stern. "Doesn't Western Union pay you a salary?"

"Yes, but not enough," the boy shrugged.

Etta's body became rigid, her voice firm. "Then look for another job. You should be ashamed of yourself—a healthy, young man like you—expecting handouts. Now you get a move on!" she ordered.

"Yes, ma'am," he said, then turned, bounded down the steps, and was soon in his car.

Etta watched the car pull away from the curb and disappear at the next corner. Suddenly, she realized that Hattie was still standing beside her.

"You're going to be late for school," she said abruptly.

"Is there anything I can do?" Hattie offered.

"No," Etta told her, "but thank you for your help. Now, you'd better go on to school. I have to call my sisters."

"I'll miss school if I can be of some help."

"That's not necessary," Etta said, opening the door. "My sisters and I will take care of everything."

2

Etta pressed the telephone tightly against her ear, and formed her words in loud, precise tones. "Operator, I want to call Mrs. Agnes Williams—3840 Front Street, in Amarillo, Texas. Her number is Randolf—RA 3 -0298."

"One moment, please," the operator's voice responded.

As the telephone blurted riveted buzzes, Etta attempted to compose her words.

A woman's voice answered.

"Agnes?" Etta said loudly, "Agnes, this is Etta."

"Etta?" her sister echoed.

"Agnes, I just got a telegram from Osawatomie. Theodore is in critical condition, it said." Etta waited briefly for an answer. "Agnes, are you there? I can't hear you."

"I'm here," she answered.

"I can't hear you, Agnes, speak up!"

"I said, I'm here!" the voice blared out.

"Now, I can hear you," Etta replied, nodding her head. "Did you hear what I said about the telegram from Osawatomie? Theodore is bad sick and they want to know if we want to see him."

Etta waited. "Agnes!" she finally scolded, "answer me!"

Her sister answered quickly, "I am sorry to hear it."

"I didn't call you to hear how sorry you were," Etta cut back. "I called to see if you will go to Osawatomie with me and Dot."

"Did Dot say she'd go?"

"I haven't called Dot, but of course, she'll go," Etta told her.

"I bet she won't," her sister retorted bluntly.

"Agnes," Etta said trying to contain her disgust, "I didn't call to argue. Will you come to Springfield and go with Dot and me to Osawatomie?"

She waited for a reply.

"Agnes, answer me!" she commanded.

"I don't know," Agnes said.

"What do you mean, you don't know? Theodore is your only brother. He's in critical condition—dying— and you don't know whether you'll go see him or not?"

"Give me time to think."

"Long distance costs money," Etta said, flatly. "You think about it and call me back!"

"Well," Agnes replied, hesitantly, "I'll have to talk

to Harry. . . ."

"Since when?" Etta asked. "You've never discussed anything with Harry since you married him."

"Well, Etta, " Agnes slowly explained, "Harry has to drive me to Springfield if I come. And you know we'll have to give a reason to the children."

"Tell the children your brother is dying and you want to see him," Etta said, impatiently.

Her sister's voice became excited. "you know I can't do that! You know I've never told them about Theodore."

"And you know what I think about that!" Etta snapped.

"If I want to protect my children from unpleasantness and any embarrassment, that's my business!" Agnes returned, quickly.

"Mike and Alice are over thirty years old. I hardly call them children," Etta said, setting her jaw. "Surely, they're old enough to hear something unpleasant by now."

"What I tell my children is my concern," Agnes replied.

"I don't care what you tell them. I just don't understand why you've always been so chicken-hearted about Theodore."

Her sister burst into tears. "I won't listen to you talk to me that way!"

"Oh, Agnes," Etta sighed, "grow up!"

Only sobs could be heard coming from the Amarillo connection.

"Agnes," Etta announced, "I'm not going to pay

money to the telephone company to hear you bawl. After you've told Harry what you're going to do and made up whatever stories you're going to tell the others, call me and tell me when you'll be here. Agnes, I'm going to hang up now. Agnes, do you hear me!"

No answer was heard, only more sobbing.

"Agnes," Etta's voice commanded, "answer me!"

Her sister's voice replied, "Yes, Etta, I'll call you back."

"When?" Etta demanded. "When will you call me back?"

"This afternoon."

"All right," Etta agreed. "I'll hang up now. Good-bye."

Etta placed the phone on the receiver. "Damn!" she said, and realizing what she had said, she put her hand over her mouth.

Etta had lost control—she knew it. That always happened with Agnes. Etta scolded herself for she had repeatedly vowed that it wouldn't happen again. But that same resolution had been made and broken many times. Agnes was a whiner. Etta had never been able to abide sniveling women or children and Agnes had been both, bursting into tears at the drop of a hat.

"Mama, Etta's being mean to me again."

"Etta! Come in here this minute!"

How well she could visualize Agnes' shriveled-up face, looking like she had bitten into a dried persimmon, crying her alligator tears.

"Etta's yanking my hair again!"

Agnes' hair—how many times had Etta been tempted to grab up the scissors and amputate the long copper strands. It was Agnes who received the compliments for its radiant color, but it was Etta who had to brush it every morning before sending the child off to school. In summer the hair turned bright orange with streaks of golden highlight forming flowing ribbons which swirled lazily against her sister's back and shoulders. But Etta never saw the beauty of it, for she was the one who had to brush it and twist it evenly into braids while Agnes whined and bawled like a sick calf.

Etta supposed that Agnes didn't give her any more trouble than Dorothy had. Dorothy had a stubborn streak as wide as a barn and would argue with a signpost, but she was never a whiner. Thank God for even small favors!

Dorothy. . . .

Etta dialed the number. She counted the rings—one, two, three, four.

"Hello," her sister's voice answered.

"Dot, this is Etta."

"Etta, how are you?"

"I'm no good, Dot," Etta said, deciding to ease into the conversation. "My ankles are swelled up 'til I can hardly walk."

"Marjorie and I started to drive over only yesterday to see you," Dorothy interjected, quickly, "but we just never got around to it. You know how it is."

"I know," Etta said with overly understanding tones. "Marjorie is good about coming to see me.

If you came over as often as your daughter, I'd have no gripes."

"Oh, Etta, I've been so busy. Marjorie has grown so I've had to let down the hems in all her dresses and now I've got to do the same thing to her school clothes in the next two weeks. Doesn't seem possible, my little Marjorie will be a junior this year. She's the last one I've got at home. When she marries, Alfred and I will be left all alone."

"How is Alfred?" Etta interrupted.

"Grouchy as a bear," Dorothy said, seriously. "Looks like they're going to make him retire next year. I don't know what he'll do if he doesn't have that feedstore to go to every morning."

"He'll adjust to it," Etta said, matter-of-factly.

Dorothy laughed. "Oh, Alfred will adjust to anything, but I wonder if I can. I don't know if I can stand him puttering around the house every day."

"What an awful thing to say!" Etta scolded her.

"Etta, you know I love Alfred, but I must have some time for myself."

Etta stopped listening to her. "I got a telegram from Osawatomie this morning."

"About Theodore?"

"Yes," Etta's voice cracked. "Dorothy, they think he's dying. The telegram said he's in critical condition."

"Well, maybe it's a blessing, poor soul," Dorothy pondered.

"Don't say such a thing!" Etta exclaimed.

"Well, what good is he to himself or anyone

else, the way he is?"

"He's our brother," Etta reminded her.

"Oh, Etta, is he really?" Dorothy replied, reflectively. "You said yourself he didn't even recognize you the last time you went there."

"I said he wouldn't believe I was *Etta*. I've changed so from what he remembered." Etta's voice hesitated. "I sent a telegram back and told them we'd come as soon as possible."

"What do you mean, *we*?"

"You and Agnes and me, of course. We're the only family Theodore has."

"Count me out," Dorothy said, abruptly. "I haven't seen him since you took him there, and I certainly don't intend to see him now."

"But you're his sister," Etta argued.

"I might as well be sister to a tree. He wouldn't even know me. He wouldn't know any of us. I tell you, Etta, this is ridiculous. It means traveling two hundred and fifty miles to Osawatomie, Kansas, to see someone who won't even know we're there."

"Oh, Dot, don't say any more," Etta gasped.

"Well, I'm not going and that's that," Dorothy replied with finality. "And mark my words, when Agnes hears about this, she'll agree with me. We've got no business going up there. We'd just be in the way. You call Agnes. She'll tell you the same thing."

"I've already called Agnes," Etta admitted.

"What did she say?" Dorothy plunged back. "What did Agnes say?"

Etta's voice revealed the disgust she felt. "She

bawled like she always does."

"I bet you got her all upset like you always do," Dorothy reprimanded. "Why didn't you call me first? Here I am in Springfield, right here in town, but do you call me first? No! You've got to call Agnes and get her all upset. And me, right here in town!"

"No more than I ever see you, you might as well live in Alaska!" Etta said, curtly.

"That's it, rub it in. I don't come over and see you often enough. You already threw that up to me. Can I help it if I'm busy and have my own family to care for? Can I help it?" Dorothy didn't wait for an answer. "If I came over every morning you'd gripe because I didn't come in the afternoon. That's all you've ever done—gripe at me and Agnes! You know what your trouble is, Etta? You're alone too much. You really should go out and look at Walnut Acres."

"You mean the *old folks' home?*" Etta bristled.

"They don't call them 'old folks' homes' anymore," Dorothy corrected her. "They're called 'rest homes.' "

"I get all the rest I need," Etta said flatly.

"But you would have company there, with people . . . well . . . your own age."

"I don't like people my own age," Etta retorted. "I see all the old people I can stand at church."

"Well, you need something to take up your time," Dorothy instructed, "instead of trying to tell me and Agnes what we should do." Her voice stopped, briefly, then she thought aloud: "I bet Agnes is trying to call me right now to tell me about it."

Etta's tone was sharp. "So you two can lick each

other's wounds."

"There you go, cutting at me again." Dorothy stopped abruptly. "What did Agnes say? Did she agree to make this ridiculous trip?"

"She couldn't say," Etta said quietly. "She's going to call me back this afternoon."

"Well," Dorothy said with certainty, "she won't go. I can tell you that. And I'm not going either. And there's no sense in you going. Theodore won't even know you're there."

Etta's answer was quiet and firm. "*I'll* know I'm there," she said.

"Do as you please," Dorothy snapped. "But don't expect me to go with you."

"All right, Dorothy, all right," Etta said, not wanting to hear any more.

"Etta, wake up to reality," her sister demanded. "That's not our brother at Osawatomie. Our brother died that hot summer day in Kansas. All that's left of our brother is a feeble idiot!"

"Oh, Dot," Etta cried out. "I won't listen to you talk that way. Theodore *is* our brother!"

"Not any more," Dorothy's voice was coldly resolute. "Not after that day. He was never our brother again. He was an infant, a grown infant. He had to be cared for and watched. God knows, he would have been better off if he had died that day. We all would have been better off. It same as killed Papa. He was never the same after it happened either. And Agnes and I had to take the brunt of it. Being laughed at and jeered at. Our lives were made miserable. We had to go to school and listen to all the remarks. Papa should have put him someplace then. And he would have, too, if he hadn't listened to you.

"But, oh, no," Dorothy continued, "you were worse than he was—'Theodore's our brother,' you said, 'we'll take care of him.' Then you married Frank and left town. But Agnes and I couldn't get away. We had to stay there and go to school and come home to Mama crying and Papa hardly ever saying a word. . . and Theodore, babbling like an idiot!"

"Dorothy, I'm not going to listen to any more!" Etta's voice forced. "I'm going to hang up!"

"Very well," Dorothy answered, "I'll talk to you later."

"With your attitude, I don't think I want to talk to you later!" Etta told her.

"Suit yourself!" Dorothy said coldly.

Etta held the phone for a moment. She looked at the black plastic mouthpiece with the drilled holes, wondering what she could say to make Dorothy reconsider. Dorothy's tightlipped stubbornness crossed her mind. Deciding there was nothing more to say, Etta placed the phone on the receiver.

For some time, Etta sat retracing the conversation in her mind. The morning sunlight streaked through the window and touched her thighs. Her hand automatically reached down and rubbed at the warmth. The wall clock chimed nine strokes. Etta looked up and became aware of the heat filling the kitchen. She stood up and walked to the window. Petey chirped as she brushed against his cage to lower the green window shade, but she paid no attention to him.

Etta proceeded to the bedroom, stopping only to pull down the blinds. Then she covered each window in the living room. Etta paused at the east window. "Hattie was right," she thought, "it will be a 'scorcher' until rain comes."

She was drawn to look at the yellow sun that pierced the clear blue sky. It glowed, like a coal, commanding her attention. Etta stared, her eyes fixed on the flaming sphere; its golden color changed to red, then glowed white. When finally she lowered the shade, white specks floated across the flat green backing. As she turned, the spots seemed to beckon before her, and began to move across the walls of the darkened room. The changing colors spun around her. Suddenly, she felt light-headed. She groped for the armchair like a blind person searching for a railing. Once she found it she sat down, fitting herself securely in the safety of its padded arms. Pressing her head against the high back, she closed her eyes. The spots swirled even faster. The whites became reds, then faded into greens and blues, and finally . . . disappeared.

Etta opened her eyes. Slowly, the objects in the darkened room became visible but she did not see them. The sound of her sister's voice echoed in her ears—"Theodore was never the same after that day," the voice kept repeating—"that day . . . that day . . . that day . . ."

That day...time and again, Etta had tried to remember every detail of that hot summer day years ago. It was August. She knew the date by rote—August 4, 1903. If there had been anything unusual about the morning, she couldn't recall it. There had been no warning of any kind...except it was hot, she remembered... *very* hot. But then, Kansas is always an oven during August. The sun scorched the plains, burning the fields of wheat brown. There was no place to escape the heat. Even the morning breeze bore its hot breath. The heat was there. She remembered the heat...she felt it now. She breathed in its stifling warmth.

She must have worked with her father in the fields that morning as she was accustomed to doing, but she couldn't recall exactly what she had done. She had searched her memory again and again, yet she couldn't reassemble the beginning hours.

Like hundreds of other mornings, she reasoned, she must have prepared breakfast—bacon, eggs, biscuits and cereal. She could remember the kitchen table; she could remember carrying water from the pump; she could remember the wood stove. Papa kindled the stove first thing every morning. It was always pitch hot by the time Etta was dressed. How old was she then? She counted back—she was twenty-two. Other girls her age were married, but she had waited. Repeatedly, Frank had asked her to marry him and she put him off. "Next year Agnes will be out of grammar school," she told him. "Then Agnes can help at home." He wouldn't wait forever, Frank had warned her, but she wasn't worried.

Twenty-two—yes, she was twenty-two that summer. Her auburn hair was so long that when it was unbraided, she could sit on it. First thing each morning, she would brush her hair and weave it into one thick braid. She pulled so tightly that it pinched her scalp, then wrapped the rope of silky braid around her head. Tortoise shell pins held it securely in place. While still in her nightgown, she would run out to the pump and splash handfuls of water on her face to wash the sleep from her eyes. How she loved the shock of the ice cold water, for it made her shiver and feel totally awake and alive.

Yes, she must have washed her face at the pump that morning. And of course, she would have dressed and cooked breakfast for everyone but her mother. Mama usually waited until the others were finished and out of the house. Once Papa was in the fields and Etta had shooed the children to their chores, Mama would dress and prepare her own breakfast. When she finished her morning meal, she would carry her cup out to the rocker on the porch. As she rocked back and forth, she would leisurely sip her coffee. On that morning everything must have been the same.

Except, while Etta prepared breakfast, she had noticed that the sack of salt was nearly empty. She decided to send Theodore to town. She made a list of other things they needed—surely she made a list for she never sent her brother on the long walk for one lone item.

Theodore was nine years old that summer. He wouldn't mind the walk—the fact was, he always looked forward to a trip to town. To him, it meant three miles of adventure. There were turtles to look for, and smooth, colored rocks to add to his prized collection. He usually came back with his pockets stuffed full of so-called treasures.

Had it been that very morning when Theodore brought a snake egg to show her? She couldn't remember. It might have been any morning, for he was forever bringing some wild thing for her to see. If it had been, she had probably scolded him. Oh, God, she hoped she had not been cross with him that morning, or scolded him, or said anything to hurt his feelings—not that morning—especially that morning.

Surely she had told him not to tarry in town and not to dawdle going or coming. Surely, she had stressed that he keep to the road and not cut across Parker Mason's farm, because Mr. Mason had often warned the children to stay off his property. Yes, she must have told him all those things, for she had repeated them on countless occasions.

It was early morning when Theodore started to town. No doubt, Etta had waved to him as he began walking up the dusty road. Perhaps she had even taken the extra time to watch the dust scatter around his bare feet. She may have watched as the sunlight glistened on his golden hair.

Etta could see him now, walking up the hill. She could describe, in detail, the faded print shirt he wore, for she had sewn it when the colors were bright and new. She had mended the shirt when it was gnawed by sharp tree branches and ragged riverbed rocks.

His faded overalls hung loosely around his muscled legs. They had been bought with plenty of room to spare for him to grow. Already, they had patches on the knees and one back pocket had been completely torn away during a "battle of honor" with J. T. Thornby—over what, she never quite knew. The pant legs were rolled halfway up his calves. Yes, Etta had watched her brother that morning as he became a speck on the long brown road. Then, together, the boy and the stretch of dirt road faded into the distance.

3

The sharp ring from the telephone interrupted the silence of Etta's darkened room. She realized it had been signaling for some time.

"Hello," she answered gruffly as she seated herself before the desk.

"Etta," the voice scolded, "where on earth have you been? I nearly rang the phone off the wall!"

It was Dorothy's voice.

"I was right here in the living room," Etta answered shortly.

"Well," her sister replied in disgust, "I dialed your number three times and I let it ring and ring."

"You must have dialed the wrong number," Etta countered. "I've been right here. If it had rung, I would have heard it." Then, to strengthen her defense, Etta added—"I may be old, but I'm not *deaf*, you know. What do you want, Dot?"

Dorothy's tones were calculated. "I just finished talking to Agnes."

Etta was familiar with her sister's approach but she decided to hear Dorothy out.

"Agnes is coming to Springfield," Dorothy informed her. "Harry said he would drive her up. But Harry said the trip to Osawatomie is out of the question. He'll have no part of it."

"Then why are they driving up?" Etta exclaimed, hoarsely.

"To be here in case we get bad news from Osawatomie, of course," Dorothy said.

"Don't you and Agnes realize," she protested, "that we've already got bad news from Osawatomie?"

"Oh, Etta," Dorothy forced her voice to sympathetic tones, "you know what I mean."

But Etta wasn't in the mood for verbal games. "You mean, Agnes wants to be here when we receive word that Theodore is *dead*."

Dorothy carefully stressed each word: "Agnes wants to be here in case we need her."

"No one needs her here," Etta cut back. "If she's not going to Osawatomie with us, we don't need her at all. Tell her to stay home!"

"I'll do no such thing!" Dorothy bristled. "Agnes wants to help. She even suggested the three of us get together and send some flowers. I told her I thought that would be a wonderful idea. Don't you?"

Etta's voice was low. "If I decide to send Theodore

anything, it'll be a smooth rock."

Dorothy's gasp was a mixture of surprised puzzle-ment and uncertain laughter. "I swear, Etta," she said, "sometimes I don't understand you at all."

"Dorothy," Etta stressed, "I need transportation to Osawatomie. If Agnes and Harry won't take me there, then you and Alfred must. Don't you understand? All this talk about flowers and waiting for another telegram is driving me straight up the wall. Some way, I have to get to Theodore. I can't let him die alone. . . . Dorothy," Etta choked, forcing the words, *"please* ask Alfred if he will drive us to Osawatomie."

"Don't you realize Alfred would have to miss work?" her sister said in disgust. "I wouldn't dare ask him to do such a thing. You don't realize how important he is at the store."

"How are they going to do without him next year after they make him retire?"

Dorothy refused to answer. "I'm not going to ask Alfred and that's that. And don't you dare ask him!" she warned.

"Then, you get ready and you and I will catch a train," Etta urged.

"And leave Alfred and Marjorie at home, alone?"

"Marjorie is sixteen. Surely she's old enough to take care of the house for a few days."

"Etta," Dorothy replied with finality, "Etta, I am *not* going to Osawatomie. And if you want my advice. . . ."

Etta didn't let her finish. "I don't want your advice, Dorothy. I'll call Robert—he'll drive me there."

"Oh," Dorothy said, changing her tone, "is Robert back in town? I didn't know that. . . ."

"Yes, he's working on the addition to the South Side Baptist Church."

"I didn't know Robert would go that close to a church without getting married," Dorothy mused.

Etta clipped her words. "That remark is uncalled for!"

"Well," Dorothy said, clearing her throat, "he has been married *eight* times."

"Six," Etta corrected her.

"Six?" Dorothy questioned, pretending, momentarily, not to remember. "Oh, yes, he just lived with those other two, didn't he? Of course, I don't blame any woman for not staying with a man who drinks."

"For your information, my son has quit drinking."

"That's what you used to say about Frank."

"Frank did quit, and you know it. During the last ten years of his life, he never drank a drop."

"Well," Dorothy said coldly, "if you're so set on going, maybe Robert will take you."

"If you're finished, Dorothy, I'm going to hang up," Etta announced.

"Wait a minute," Dorothy said quickly, then her voice resumed her saddened tones. "Etta, what shall we do about the flowers?"

Considering the conversation closed, Etta slammed the phone against the receiver. She sat there, stiffly, holding her hand on the phone as it began to ring again. Certain that it was Dorothy calling back to rebuke her for hanging up, Etta refused to answer.

When finally the ringing ceased, Etta raised the receiver and dialed.

"Hello, Jessie. This is Mrs. Pearson," Etta told her. "When Robert comes home, will you have him give me a call?"

"He's here now," Jessie said. "He's outside."

"Why isn't he at work?" she asked with concern. "He hasn't been drinking again, has he?"

"No, he hasn't had a drink in two weeks, Mrs. Pearson," Jessie soothed her. "The car had a flat tire this morning when he went out. He started to put the spare on, but it was flat too. So he called into work and took the day off."

"Oh, I'm so glad—not that he's got a flat tire, but that he's not been drinking. Jessie, I pray every night that he doesn't start again."

Jessie's tone was in agreement. "It's a sickness, Mrs. Pearson."

"It's in his blood, Jessie," Etta considered. "His father was a drinker and his uncles drank. It's in his blood. I worry about him and I know you do, too."

"Yes," Jessie replied, "but it's something he has to work out. Wait a minute, Mrs. Pearson, I'll call him to the phone."

"No, don't bother him while he's fixing the tire," Etta said, quickly. "But as soon as he's finished, have him call me, will you?"

"Is there anything wrong?" Jessie questioned.

"It's a family problem," Etta told her.

Jessie understood. Considering the high mortality rate of his other marriages, being Robert's wife hardly offered her little more than temporary courtesies. It certainly didn't place her in a position to share family confidences.

"I'll have him call you right away," she said.

"Thank you, Jessie," Etta told her. "If you're finished, I'll hang up now. Good-bye."

At last Etta's hopes rose. Robert's happening to be home was the first piece of luck she had had all morning. He would take her to Theodore, she knew it. And he's stopped drinking—"Thank God," she sighed.

Once more, she sat in the overstuffed chair near the desk to wait for his call. She looked up at the clock—it was ten thirty. Leaning her head against the back of the chair, she closed her eyes and drew a deep breath.

Where's Theodore?" her mother had called from the porch.

"I sent him to town," Etta recalled telling her.

"Etta," her mother called to her again, "come help me carry my rocker out under the shade tree. It's getting too hot up here on the porch."

She helped her mother lift the heavy rocker. Together, they carried it down the wooden steps into the yard, and placed it in the shade of the giant oak.

"It's so hot I can hardly get my breath," her mother moaned, placing her hand to her breast as she took several quick gasps of air. The thin woman sat down in the rocker. "I wish Theodore would come on. The sun's so hot it'll roast him alive."

"He's hardly had time to get to town," Etta reasoned, "but he should be back before noon." However, she later recalled glancing up at the road to see if he might be coming. The road lay bare with the sun bleaching the dust.

Throughout the morning, her mother called to her many times. "Theodore is not home yet," she would say. "When is Theodore coming home?"

Mama always did go on so. Her sense of time was never accurate.

At first Etta answered, "He hasn't had time to walk all the way to town and back yet."

By midday, her answers changed to, "He should be home any minute."

Her mother scooted her chair to the edge of the shaded grass to gain a better view. The road stretched out over the hill, naked of any traveler.

From time to time, Etta stopped her work in the cornfield to crane her neck and look up toward the road. Her thoughts turned from, "He's dawdling, looking for rocks again," to "I'll give him what for when he gets home."

Then finally late in the afternoon, Etta became concerned. Her mother watched as the young girl walked up the dusty road to the crest of the hill. Etta could still feel the heat of the dust between her toes and how her bare feet smarted against the hot rocks. In her mind, she could still see herself standing alone in the road, looking toward town. As far as she could see, the plains were without motion. There was no hint of a breeze anywhere. The whole earth seemed baked by the afternoon sun.

"Where is that boy!" she wondered aloud.

The ring of the telephone slashed through the years. Etta answered it before the first signal was completed.

"Hello," she said. "Yes, Robert, I've been waiting for you to call." Her voice became low. "I need your help, son. I got a telegram from the State Hospital at Osawatomie this morning. Your Uncle Theodore is bad sick. They think he's dying. Robert, I've got to go there to see him before he's gone. Could you drive me to Osawatomie?"

Robert didn't hesitate. "Of course, I'll take you, Mother. How soon can you be ready?"

Etta was so relieved by his answer that tears suddenly filled her eyes and she had difficulty speaking. "I think I can be ready in an hour," she finally said.

"I can't leave quite that soon, Mom," he told her. "I wouldn't dare start out with the tires I've got on the car. Tell you what. I'll drive downtown and buy a couple of recaps and have them put on. Let's see, it's noon now. You be ready about three o'clock and I'll be out to pick you up."

"Oh, Robert," Etta said excitedly, "I'll fix some supper and we can eat together before we leave."

"You'll do no such thing," he insisted. "No, ma'am, don't you fix a thing. You take your time and pretty yourself up and you and I will eat at the best diner on the highway."

"But it costs too much to eat out," she argued

halfheartedly.

"Now, don't you worry your pretty little head about money. I'll stop by the construction site and pick up my paycheck. Why, we'll have money to burn," her son laughed. "We may stop at several diners on the way. We could have soup at one, a salad at another, and a steak in still another. We could end up having pie a la mode a hundred miles away from our soup."

"Oh, son, you do go on so," Etta chuckled.

"And when we get tired, we'll stop at the fanciest motel on the road. And, with you all dolled up, I bet I'll have to hand the clerk an extra fiver to let us in. Why, he'll never believe you're my mother. He'll think we're out on a lark."

Etta laughed heartily, ashamed of herself for seeing humor in such an idea. "Robert, you're sinful in your thoughts. You're just like your father, so I guess you come by it natural."

"It's a date then," he kidded her. "I'll pick you up at three o'clock. Shall I stop down the street or shall I come straight up to the front door for all the neighbors to see?"

Etta laughed until she could hardly answer. "You drive right up to the front door. We'll give 'em all something to talk about."

"I'll see you at three then," he said.

As Etta placed the phone on the receiver, she found herself laughing again. "You old fool," she said.

4

The suitcase was spread open on the bed. Neat stacks of stockings and undergarments had been placed beside it. Selected dresses were suspended on hangers in the doorway.

The front door opened. "Anybody home?" a voice called in.

Etta recognized the voice.

"I'm here in the bedroom, Dot," Etta answered.

Dorothy's hands parted the dresses that hung in the doorway to the bedroom and she peeked her head in. "What on earth's going on here?" she questioned, opening her eyes, widely, attempting to effect an expression of innocent curiosity.

"I'm packing," Etta said to the open room, not bothering to turn around.

Dorothy edged her way past the curtain of clothing and seated herself on the stool in front of the dressing table. She could never resist posing herself before a mirror, twisting her hair with her fingers and pressing tight curls toward her face. When pursing her lips and raising her eyebrows before a mirror, Dorothy felt she appeared quite elegant.

"Did you get in touch with Robert?" she asked coyly.

Etta still didn't turn toward her sister. "Yes, I did," she answered.

Another face peeked through the hanging dresses.

"Aunt Etta."

Etta turned toward the door. "There's my pretty girl," she said brightly. "Marjorie, I wondered where you were."

Marjorie wrapped her arms around her aunt, kissing her on the cheek. "Guess who drove the car all the way over here?"

"The Duke of Windsor!" Etta kidded.

"*I* did!" Marjorie squealed. "Just got my driver's license."

"Good for you," Etta chuckled. "Sixteen and a driver. Your mother isn't losing a child, she's gaining a chauffeur."

Marjorie was pleased with herself. "I thought fifteen would never end. Honestly, I thought I'd die fifteen."

"Marjorie, don't be so silly," her mother scolded her daughter's reflection in the mirror.

Etta motioned with her head. "If you look under the cloth on the kitchen table you'll find a jar of cookies."

"Oatmeal or sugar?"

"Since when did you get so particular?" Etta laughed.

The young girl let her hands float in the air, tiptoeing in animated ballet steps to the kitchen door. "Since I became sixteen," she cooed in affected hautiness.

Etta laughed again while Dorothy chose to ignore everything except the curl at her left temple.

"When are you leaving?" she pursued in a forced, casual tone.

Etta resumed her packing. "Robert's going to be here at three."

"Oh, that's nice. I was afraid you might not be able to get in touch with him since he wasn't at work," Dorothy said in overly concerned tones.

Etta turned straight toward her sister. "How did you know Robert wasn't at work?" she asked.

"We happened to drive past the South Side Church on our way here. We didn't see Robert *anywhere*. So I had Marjorie stop the car and I called to one of the workmen. He said Robert hadn't shown up for work this morning. So, naturally, I thought he had— well, you know—"

"You thought he had what?" Etta pressed.

"Well, you know," Dorothy said raising her eyebrows, "if he hadn't shown up at work, I just naturally supposed he was tipping the bottle again."

Etta placed her hands firmly on her hips. "I told you Robert has quit drinking."

"Well, you can never tell," Dorothy snipped.

Marjorie came back into the bedroom munching

cookies and carrying a glass of milk. "Oh, Aunt Etta, I was so embarrassed when Mother called to those workmen like she did. Since I was the driver, they looked right down at me. They must have thought I had called to them. Some of them whistled— I could have died! Right in front of the church and all!"

"Nonsense," her mother said. "Men can always tell a lady when they see one."

"Well, they didn't whistle like they thought I was a lady," Marjorie mused.

"Maybe they were whistling at your mother," Dorothy said, raising her chin, glancing at her profile in the mirror.

"Maybe *your mother* was the one they couldn't tell was a *lady*," Etta couldn't resist saying.

Etta looked at Marjorie and they burst into laughter.

Dorothy saw no humor in the comment and decided to change the subject. "Well," she said, "I guess there's nothing I can say or do to persuade you not to make this ridiculous trip."

Etta turned back to her packing. "No, Dot, there isn't."

"It's a real shame—you leaving with Agnes coming in tomorrow morning. After all, we haven't seen her in months."

Etta's voice deepened. "And neither one of you has seen Theodore in years!"

Dorothy glanced at Marjorie. "Well," she exclaimed, "you know my views on that!"

Etta turned to face her. "Yes, I do. But I can't say that I understand them. Theodore is your brother and you're willing to sit back and let him die alone."

"He wouldn't know the difference," Dorothy insisted.

"But you do, Dorothy," Etta retorted. "*You* know the difference. And I must say, I'm ashamed."

Dorothy didn't answer. She sat quietly, looking at the floor.

Etta wrapped stockings into a roll and placed them in the suitcase.

"It's not right," Etta said near a whisper. "It's not right for a man to die alone. His life must be worth something. I can't let it pass away without notice. It simply isn't right for a man to die alone."

Not knowing what to say, Marjorie sat in silence. She couldn't look at either of the women. She was deeply touched but afraid if she tried to say a word, she might laugh. "Why is it," she wondered, "in times of crisis, I get the giggles. I mustn't laugh now!" she ordered herself.

Finally Dorothy spoke up. "Well, I'll have no part in it. I claim no responsibility and neither does Agnes!"

"That's just it, Dorothy," Etta said with bitterness creeping into her voice. "You and Agnes *never* claimed any responsibility. When Papa died, neither of you claimed any responsibility for either Mama or for Theodore. They came to my house to live. I cared for them. You never offered to take them, even for a week, to relieve me. Neither did Agnes. You both had homes of your own and you could have helped. But no, they were *your* homes, and you guarded them with stone walls and cold disregard for others.

"In those last months," she continued, "when Mama lay dying, did either of you offer to help? No! It was all too unpleasant for you or Agnes to bear. But Etta's strong—she's made of sturdy stuff. She's fit to take care of Mama and carry her slops. Your children couldn't be neglected but my children didn't matter! I could take care of my house and children and Theodore and Mama, God bless her sweet life. Etta's responsible. If Etta will do it, let her! Let Etta do it!" She brushed the tears from her cheeks, angry that she had allowed them to escape from her eyes.

"And after Mama died," she continued "the three of us could have kept Theodore. Frank told me that if you and Agnes would only keep him three months out of the year, he wouldn't force me to put him in the State Hospital. Only three months! Oh, my God, Dorothy, three months of responsibility between you and Agnes. Forty-five days apiece. Surely forty-five days of helping wasn't too much to ask. And you both turned me down flat! I pleaded with Frank—you know how I pleaded with him! But it was no use. No one offered to share the responsibility!"

Etta turned away, facing the wall. "Then I had to pack Theodore's things and tell him we were taking a trip. He never once guessed that I would take him someplace and leave him—that I wouldn't be bringing him back. I had to take him to Osawatomie to leave him in a strange place with strangers. Oh, Theodore!" she cried, sitting down on the edge of the bed. Her hand searched for her apron pocket and pulled out her handkerchief to dry her eyes.

"So, don't talk to me about responsibility!" she said. "You don't know the first thing about it."

"Marjorie," Dorothy said briskly, as she stood up, "we had best go home."

Marjorie bent down and kissed her aunt good-bye, then left the room.

"Tell Robert I said, 'Hello,' " Dorothy told her. "And be careful on the highway. They drive like idiots today."

She waited, but Etta didn't answer. Finally Dorothy walked to the bed and bent over, giving Etta a quick kiss on the side of the face.

Etta turned, looked straight into her sister's eyes, and clenching her teeth, said, "Judas Iscariot!"

Dorothy grabbed her purse from the dresser top, and without another word left the house.

Etta sat there, not moving. She heard the car doors shut, the motor start and the car pull out of the driveway. At last, she glanced up. She was alone in the room.

She tried to retrace the conversation with Dorothy, hoping her words had been convincing. But the words were muffled. Her memory guided her, instead, to the vision of a young woman standing alone on the plains, silhouetted against the orange horizon.

Voices crept into her mind. "Where is Theodore?" her mother called as Etta came back to the gate. "Did you see Theodore?"

The girl shook her head, not stopping to talk. She made her way straight to the fields to tell her father that Theodore had not returned.

As they rode toward town in the buckboard, Etta and her father looked all directions.

"Why, yes, Theodore was in here early this morning," Mr. Welles, the storekeeper, told them, "but he wasn't here long—said he was told to get straight home."

"But did you see him leave town?" her father asked.

Mr. Welles walked to the window and considered it. "Yep, he walked right down the street there. He didn't stop for nothing."

There were three farms between town and home. Etta and her father stopped at each one to inquire if Theodore had been seen.

Mrs. Simonsen said that she had waved to the boy from the backyard as she was hanging out the wash. Yes, Mrs. Simonsen remembered Theodore was walking in the direction of his home, and that it had been before noon, she thought.

Mr. and Mrs. Hulings said they had not seen Theodore either going or coming from town, but Mr. Hulings recalled, "My hounds barked and carried on something awful this morning—the first time was early morning, then again just before noon. It might have been Theodore who riled them so."

The Hulings said they hadn't noticed anyone else on the road all day.

The sun had settled low in the western sky by the time Etta's father pulled the buckboard to a stop in front of Parker Mason's house. Mason and his wife had no children. They lived alone and discouraged visitors from stopping by. Mrs. Mason called to her husband and he came around the side of the house.

Etta's father asked if either of them had seen Theodore that day.

Parker Mason was a surly man. Etta had never liked him. She wondered if the man ever bathed, for he always smelled rank. And his attitudes were even nastier than his clothing. He was abrupt with adults and hateful with children. Etta's back tightened against the wooden seat of the buckboard as Mr. Mason came near.

"I thought you'd be comin' around," he said gruffly. "Haven't seen your brat since I caught him trespassin' 'round my barn this morning."

It was Etta who first noticed that Parker Mason carried a brown paper sack in his clenched hand.

"He ran off and left these groceries," Mason grunted, holding up the bag. "If I've told your young'uns not to cut 'cross my property once, I've told 'em a hundred times—but this morning, there he was again out there behind my barn. I see'd him. I told him to get and he took off running like a skeered jackrabbit."

Etta's father said he would see to it that it didn't happen again and tried to explain that he was worried because Theodore had not arrived home.

"The way he shot out of here, he shoulda been home in no time," Mason replied. "I bet he won't trespass around my barn no more. I scared him good and proper this time. He was 'lookin' for rocks,' says he. Yeah, rocks! 'In a pig's eye—rocks,' says I—'I've heard cock and bull stories before,' I told him. Cuttin' 'cross my property like he owned it. But that's one kid who ain't gonna bother me no more."

Etta's father's body stiffened. His voice tightened. "Which way did the boy run?" he asked.

Mason turned, and raising his arm, pointed, "Straight 'cross the field toward your house."

Etta's father climbed down from the buckboard and told her to drive down the road while he cut across the field to search for Theodore.

"Ain't you even gonna ask my permission?" the man wanted to know.

He walked to Parker Mason and stopped directly in front of him, and took the sack from his hand. In quiet, almost whispered tones, he told the man, "If that boy is hurt in any way, you're going to answer to me."

Parker Mason stepped aside to allow her father to pass. Mason waited until Etta's father walked a distance into the field before calling out, "Don't you ever come back on my property, makin' threats at me. I'll get the sheriff after you, do you hear? And keep your brats to home!"

Etta turned the buckboard around and started it toward the road. She held the horse to a slow walk, trying to keep the wagon even with her father's strides as he crossed the field.

The sun loomed like a ball of fire on the western horizon. Her father's silhouette was momentarily swallowed in its glare. Etta held her hand over her eyes and squinted, trying to see him. Blinded by the light, she caught fleeting glimpses of the search. Then, Etta heard her father call, or she thought she had heard him. She pulled back on the reins and brought the horses to a halt. She jumped down from the buckboard and climbed over the fence. She stopped and raised her hands to shield her eyes. Then she heard her father call again. Blindly, she ran toward the sound of his voice, feeling neither the rocks nor the heat of the dirt under her feet.

"Papa, where are you?" she cried.

Suddenly, it seemed that the earth had stopped. She stood looking at her father as he bent down before her.

"Fetch Doc Marshall as fast as you can," her father told her. "I'll carry Theodore home."

She watched as he carefully lifted the boy into his arms.

"Hurry, girl!" he commanded.

Etta raced back toward the buckboard. *He must be dead! Theodore must be dead! No, if he was dead,* she argued, *Papa wouldn't have sent me for the doctor.* But her brother hadn't moved. Her father had lifted him as he might pick up some twisted rag doll. Then she realized she had never seen tears on her father's face before. The thought of it made her own eyes suddenly fill as she ran toward the road.

Etta stood up. "I won't think about it anymore!" she declared. "Not now. I can't!"

She took the dresses from the hangers in the doorway, folded them and placed them in the suitcase.

5

Etta had just finished packing the suitcase when she heard the first rumble of thunder. She raised the shade to survey the northwest horizon. The clouds had swollen, filling the sky with ominous grays. The thunder increased and soon the first drops of rain steamed on the hot pavement.

"Good thing Hattie listened to me," she said to the empty room.

The prospect of a journey began to excite her. The thoughts of Theodore had given way to the adventure of dining in restaurants and staying in motels. And she would be with her son.

She squeezed herself into her girdle, pulled the zipper through its metal course, and hooked it securely. At last, she took a deep breath; the air filled her lungs for only a moment and was forced out of her body by the rigid garment. Standing before the mirror, she surveyed her silhouette. How often had she been told she had grown old gracefully? *Lies!* she thought, *Lies!* No one grows old gracefully—they just grow old.

The figure Etta saw in the mirror was not transformed by the bone stays and elastic sides. Her body was still barrel-shaped and she knew it. This was the form she had expected to see in the mirror and she was not foolish enough to be convinced that she should find pleasure at her appearance. She remembered a time when her husband could put his hands about her waist with thumbs and index fingers touching. Then, her young legs had been lean and muscled; now, they were trunks of flesh with swollen ankles. Her feet had never been small. Even as a girl, her wide feet were her shame. In hot Kansas summers, as she had worked in the fields, her feet were bare. Uninhibited by shoes, they had broadened and spread beyond their natural size.

Etta would never forget the first time she had seen Frank Pearson. Even if she had met him at a less exciting event, he would have caught her attention.

It was at the Fall Barn Dance. Crowds of people traveled for miles to come to the Coffeyville Harvest Day Celebration. Etta had been to barn dances before, but this was a special occasion. She had recently turned sixteen, and for the first time she was allowed to mingle with the adults and permitted to dance with a member of the opposite sex. She would always remember two things about that night. First, she had purposely sashayed past the stalls where the younger girls stood giggling as they watched and mimicked the grownups dancing. She couldn't have cared less about seeing the silly girls, but she wanted to make certain that they saw her and were aware of her graduation from the sidelines.

The second event of the evening was seeing the young fiddle player who called the squares. She had never seen anyone like him before. At nineteen, Frank Pearson was prematurely white-headed. His olive skin darkened beneath the shock of snow-white hair and his teeth brightened his infectious smile. He stood tall and straight and his fiddle seemed a part of his nature. He held the fiddle with a firm, masterful grip, raking his bow across the strings like a saw cutting deep into wood.

Etta knew that the young man was a bricklayer by trade. He had traveled across the state of Kansas with his three brothers to work in the construction of banks, churches, and city halls.

As he stood before her, dressed in a plaid shirt and weathered britches, Etta envisioned him as the architect of cities. Her face flushed every time she neared the stage. Her body grew warm. Her feelings were too intense for her to be outwardly subtle. Her eyes couldn't leave the young man with the fiddle in his hands.

The young fiddler was the talk of the dance and when he announced he'd play "The Devil's Dream," the crowd gathered close to the stage. His bow cut across the strings in a low hoedown rhythm and soon increased in momentum to the shrill, frantic intensity of the devil's evil laugh. The crowd tapped their feet and clapped their hands. And the fiddler laughed, oh, how he laughed, at the crowd's reaction.

Etta saw how the other girls swarmed to the stage, gushing compliments and heaving sighs. *Nothing but a bunch of sillies*, she thought, wishing he would notice her.

For days after the dance, she thought of little except the white-haired fiddler. She hummed "The Devil's Dream," crescendoing her voice to a high, quivering pitch, imitating the sounds of the violin. She wondered if she would ever see him again. She didn't have long to wait.

The next Sunday, they met at church. Somehow Etta knew the young man would be there. That morning, she had brushed her hair until her head was sore, and then had sprinkled water over her auburn tresses, pressing in deeper waves. She tied a blue sash tightly to accentuate her trim waist and full bosom.

When she saw Frank in church, she took special care to stand where the young man couldn't see her feet. But Frank Pearson never looked at her feet—all he could see was the girl with large, smiling eyes. He had come to church that Sunday with the express purpose of seeing her again. And he returned Sunday after Sunday for the same reason. In a matter of weeks, he was invited to the farm for dinner. Together, Etta and Frank walked through the fields and down by the riverbanks, sharing those quiet Sunday afternoons—they were in love.

With the coming of winter and the completion of the brickwork on the Farmer's Bank in Coffeyville, Frank returned with his brothers to their home in Chanute, Kansas, some forty-five miles away. They exchanged letters and Etta longed for spring to see Frank again. But with the coming of the season, the best-paying construction work was in Topeka, so Frank and his brothers spent the summer working in the capital city. She pictured, in her mind, the girls in Topeka, giggling and sighing as he fiddled "The Devil's Dream." When would another brick building be started in Coffeyville, she wondered? Topeka—250 miles. It might as well have been a thousand.

Each summer, the letters came from different places—Salina, Hutchinson, Topeka, Kansas City. Each year, he seemed to be traveling farther away. Time after time, his letters asked her to come to him and they would be married.

Every spring and fall, he would journey to the farm, trying to convince her. Each time she had made her excuses: she was needed at home, her mother was sick and the children required her care. Each time, she had put him off to the next changing season. And with each new season, new reasons postponed their plans.

"If I had it all to do over again," she said to the mirror...then hesitated..."I wouldn't want to do it all over again," she said curtly. "What's done is done."

Etta picked up the comb and brought it to her head. Now her hair had become completely white, but she still remembered when it was a soft auburn and sunlight had danced in it. She had never neglected its care; her hair was brushed morning and night. She had caressed her hair as she brushed with hard, disciplined strokes and watched it wave and touch her shoulders. Then, as the years wore on, she saw its color fade until, at last, she loathed the sight of it. No longer could she endure watching the brush streak through the fading color. She hated those in-between years when her hair progressively dimmed from auburn to gray—a dull, indiscriminate mixture. At last, when the color became stark white, her vanity returned. Once each week she rinsed her hair in lemon juice to enhance that whiteness. But she kept her hair cut short in artificial permanent waves. Arthritis made long sessions of brushing and arranging it impossible.

As Etta looked in the mirror, her face was now unrecognizable to her. True, she had watched the wrinkles etch across her skin and she had been aware as the muscles softened and began to hang in soft, lazy pouches. But she didn't remember exactly when her own face became a stranger. All she could recall was that one morning, the mirror reflected unfamiliar features. Now, she saw an old woman looking back at her in the glass. It was Mrs. Pearson, but it was no longer Etta.

The rain beat against the windowpanes. By two-thirty in the afternoon, it appeared as dark as night outside. Etta could see only a misty glow of streetlights through the sheets of rain. By three o'clock, the rain had slackened to a drizzle.

Etta carried her suitcase to the front porch. The rain had cooled the earth. The trees glistened with reflective pellets of water, and the street had been washed clean. She moved her rocker closer to the bannister and sat down to wait for Robert. He would be there by three. He had promised.

The drops of rain seemed to count out the passing minutes. Then, the minutes became an hour. Shortly after four o'clock, Etta saw Hattie's gray Volkswagen pull into her driveway. She wished she could hide.

She knew that Hattie would soon be running over to her house and Etta simply didn't want to talk with anyone, let alone someone who wasn't in the family. "Oh, Robert, hurry up. If only you would get here before she comes trotting over."

Too late. Holding her umbrella aloft, Hattie alternated her strides, taking little steps, then giant steps, trying to miss the puddles on the sidewalk.

"You were right," Hattie exclaimed, stepping up on the front porch. "I'm glad I took your advice. It was pouring cats and dogs when I got out of school."

Etta forced a smile.

Hattie looked at her. "Are you all right, Mrs. Pearson?"

"I'm fine," she answered. "I'm just waiting for my son, Robert," she said, pointing toward her suitcase. "He's going to drive me to Osawatomie."

"Oh, that's good," Hattie replied. "Are you leaving soon?"

"Any minute," Etta answered. "Just as soon as he

gets here. We're going to eat at a restaurant on the way."

"Oh, you'll enjoy that," Hattie said. "Have you heard any more about your brother?"

"No," Etta replied. "I'm sure I would have heard if he had taken for the worse—bad news travels fast."

"Will you drive all night or . . . ?"

"Look Hattie," Etta interrupted, "I know you mean well, but I don't want to answer any more questions."

"Oh, I am sorry, Mrs. Pearson," she said quietly. "I was only trying to help. I don't want to be a bother."

Etta looked up. "You're not being a bother, Hattie. It's just me. I'm fit to be tied."

"I know you must be worried about your brother."

"Yes, I am," she said. "And I can't get anybody to move. That's what upsets me the most. All the calling around, trying to get people to take me—having to listen to all their milquetoast excuses. All that just riles my temper. But what makes me sorer than anything is being old. If something like this had happened ten years ago, or even five, why I wouldn't have called any of them for transportation. I would have called and said right out, 'I'm going to Osawatomie. If you want to go too, fine. If you don't, I'll see you when I get back.'

"You know what all this reminds me of?" Etta continued laughing halfheartedly. "It reminds me of the story I used to tell to my children about the chicken. I can't think of the name—the one that said, 'Who will plant the wheat?' 'Not I,' said the pig. 'Not I,' said the cow. And some other animal said the same thing. And so the chicken—whatever her name was—said, 'Then I'll do it myself,' and she did. That's what I'd like to tell them all—'Go to the devil! I'll do it myself!'" Realizing what she had said, she laughed, "I'm sorry, Hattie."

"That's all right, Mrs. Pearson. 'A little devil now and then cleans out the system,' my mother used to say."

"It certainly does," Etta said. "I feel better already. I know who it was," she said suddenly, raising her hand with the index finger extended. "The Little Red Hen. She didn't have a name—that's why I couldn't think of it."

"That's right," Hattie agreed. "I used to get her mixed up with Chicken Little."

"Not me," Etta said. "Chicken Little always reminded me of my sister, Agnes, running around with her hair on fire, yelling, 'The sky is falling, the sky is falling!'"

Now, they both laughed.

Etta stopped laughing when she saw a car turn the corner at the end of the block. Both she and Hattie watched as it passed the house.

"It's not him," Etta said, dejectedly.

"Would you like for me to sit with you until he comes?"

"No," Etta replied, shaking her head, "you haven't even had your supper."

"I don't mind."

"I know you don't," Etta said, "but to tell you the truth, I'd really rather sit here by myself. I don't feel much like talking."

"I understand," Hattie told her. "I'll be going, but if you need me, you be sure to call."

"I will."

Hattie reached over and patted the woman's hand. "Hope you have a safe trip."

"Thank you," Etta said.

Raising her umbrella overhead, Hattie stepped down off the porch.

"Hattie," Etta called, "thank you. You're a good neighbor. I like you."

"I like you too, Mrs. Pearson," she replied and hurried across the yard and into her house.

"Hattie's a good person," Etta said aloud to herself, "but a bit dull at times . . . but then, who am I to talk? I'm no Albert Einstein myself."

She looked toward the street hoping she might see Robert's car. Nothing.

Waiting. I hate the waiting," Etta had said, looking up at her father. "And the not knowing makes it even worse."

She removed the warm cloth from her brother's forehead. "It feels like it's been on the stove," she noted. After wringing the cloth out in the basin, she wiped the boy's fevered face again.

Theodore hadn't moved since her father had carried him home. Etta thought he had blinked his eyes while being examined, but the doctor insisted that was only wishful thinking. Doc Marshall had stayed through the night and when he left, he had told her father he didn't know if Theodore would be better or not—that anyone's guess was as good as his.

"Thought he was a goner for sure when I first saw him," the doctor said. "Didn't think he'd make it through the night. But he's still here. Probably had more to do with your prayers and Etta's than anything I did.

"Sunstrokes are queer things," he said, bringing a match out and striking it against the fence post. "They just seem to cook the brain." He took several puffs at his pipe, lighting it. "Sometimes, they kill the victim right then and there. And sometimes, the person gets up in a few minutes, shakes the dust off his clothes and goes back to whatever he was doing before it hit him. Yet sometimes, they just lie, unconscious for days, like Theodore is now."

"But he'll come out of it, won't he?" Etta asked, hoping he would agree.

"He might," the doctor replied, considering his words. "He might wake up tomorrow morning, hungry as a bear and raring to go. Or it might be a week. I've even seen them stay that way for months. Sometimes they don't wake up at all."

The doctor looked straight at Etta. "But Theodore's a strong boy, and he's young—that's to his credit. The main thing you can do is try to keep his fever down. If we can break the fever in the next few days, he's got a chance."

"But what if it takes weeks, or even longer?" Etta's father asked.

The doctor removed the pipe from his mouth. "If

it takes weeks or longer, you had best pray that he doesn't wake up, because chances are, he wouldn't ever be the same."

"What do you mean?" Etta wanted to know.

"In the head," he answered, pointing his pipe at his temple. "Sunstrokes affect people in much the same way other strokes do. Sometimes they can't walk. Some people can't talk. And sometimes the stroke affects their minds, and they can't think right— you know what I mean?"

"But that won't happen to Theodore, will it?" Etta said quickly.

"Let's pray it doesn't," Doc Marshall replied quietly. "He's sure a fine looking boy."

As Etta and her father walked back toward the house, she said, "I ain't gonna cry 'til Theodore gets well."

Her father put his arms around her, but he offered no answer.

"Theodore will be all right, I know it!" she said.

But even as she spoke, she was afraid that she was wrong.

To Etta, the days that followed seemed to blend together. In reality, the hours dragged slowly by, but in her memory, they blurred and raced.

Doc Marshall came to the house regularly. She and her father kept replacing the warm towels with cool, wet ones. Her brother's face and eyelids—even his tongue—were blistered from the prolonged exposure in the sun. They watched . . . and they waited.

For days, Etta's father rarely left the boy's bed—he

sat quietly, patting his son's hand. Etta could remember entering the room numerous times, but she could never remember leaving it. She must have done other chores— the cows had to be milked and meals must have been prepared—but Etta could not remember doing any of those things. "Where were Agnes and Dot?" she later wondered, for she couldn't recall even seeing them during that time. Etta could remember her mother crying and walking to the bedroom door, refusing to enter. And she would always see her father sitting, silently, looking with pleading eyes toward Doc Marshall, hoping for some reassurance that the boy would live.

Late in the night of the fourth day, Theodore made some mumbling sounds, then became quiet again.

On the seventh day, his fever lowered from 105 degrees to 101, and his breathing seemed closer to normal.

Finally, during the morning hours of the tenth day, the boy began making sounds in his sleep. Late in the afternoon, he suddenly sat straight up in bed and cried out, "Don't let him cut off my ears! Help me! Somebody help me!"

Etta grabbed the boy in her arms and held him tightly, trying to comfort him.

"You're home, honey," she said. "No one is going to hurt you. Papa's here and Etta's here. We won't let anyone hurt you."

When Etta looked up, she saw her father standing in the doorway. She hoped that he hadn't heard what her brother had said, but she knew he had, and her body suddenly filled with terror.

From the bedroom window, she watched as her father crossed the backyard and stopped at the fence. He stayed there until Doc Marshall came by shortly before dark.

The doctor asked Etta to leave the room while he examined the boy. Her father came back in the house and they waited together in the living room. Finally, the bedroom door opened and Doc Marshall came out and sat down.

"He's better, isn't he?" Etta urged.

"I think the crisis is over," the doctor replied, nodding his head. "He's a bit weak, but I think he's going to live."

"Thank God," Etta's father said quietly.

The doctor waited. "He's talking a little now, but it is a bit difficult to understand what he's saying."

"But he *is* going to be all right, isn't he?" her father asked.

"I don't know," he answered.

"What do you mean?" her father pressed.

"I can't tell," the doctor said. "The slurred speech may just be temporary. . . ."

"But then it might not?" her father interrupted.

"It might not," the doctor replied carefully.

"But his thinking isn't hurt any, is it?" her father asked, leaning closer. "Theodore's always been a real smart boy. Etta taught him the alphabet before he was three years old. Why he could read right well and count to a hundred before he ever went to school.

There ain't nothing wrong with him that way, is there?"

"I hope not," the doctor answered.

"But," her father stopped, then started again, "but you think there might be?"

"I think we should prepare ourselves, just in case."

Etta's father's hand raised up and slowly rubbed his forehead. "But that wouldn't be right," he said. "He ain't even ten years old yet. His life's hardly started. It wouldn't be right for him to be afflicted like that."

"I could be wrong," the doctor said.

"But you don't think you are, do you?" her father asked.

"No," the doctor said quietly. "Maybe if we could have broken the fever sooner . . ."

"It weren't no fever that put that boy in bed," her father said deliberately. "It was that bastard up the road, Parker Mason, that skeered him out of his wits!"

"Now, John, don't you start flying' off like that," the doctor advised. "That incident with Mason might not have anything to do with it. It might have happened anyway. Why Theodore might have already had a fever when he started to town. There's no way of knowing. You can't tell about sunstrokes— they just seem to hit people out of the blue."

"Especially if they're scared half to death!"

"Now, you don't know that, John," the doctor replied. "I tell you, Parker Mason feels real bad about Theodore. He stops me every day in front of his farm and asks about the boy. He's real upset."

"Not half as upset as he's gonna be when I get finished with him," Etta's father said.

"I don't want to hear you talking that way," Doc Marshall said firmly. "Just calm yourself. You have enough trouble here without going out looking for more. Now, John, I want you to promise me that you won't go stirring up anything with Parker Mason until all of this has died down. You've got all you can handle here. That boy's health isn't out of the woods yet. He's going to need a lot of carin' for. You get him on his feet again and if you like, I'll go over to the Mason farm with you and help you come to some kind of an understanding. But I don't want to hear of you making any more threats. Are you listening to me, John?"

"I'll do whatever's best for Theodore," her father finally replied.

"If you mean that," the doctor told him, "you'll stay right here and take care of him."

"Yessir," her father said, nodding his head.

"Good," the doctor closed the subject. "Etta," he said, turning to her, "you keep pouring plenty of liquids in that boy and start feeding him some soup. He's got to have some nourishment."

"I will," she said.

"Now then," Doc Marshall said, standing up, "I'd better hurry over to the Carey's place. Mrs. Carey is about to deliver her seventh. If I'm not there in time, she and Bert will take care of everything themselves and I'll be out two quarts of raspberry preserves. And you know, next to Etta's, Mrs. Carey makes the best raspberry preserves in the whole county."

Etta forced a smile. "I'll help you carry your things to the buggy," she said.

While her father went into the bedroom to sit with Theodore, Etta walked out to the gate with Doc Marshall.

"I want you to keep an eye on your father," the doctor said seriously. "This thing with Parker Mason really has me troubled. Don't you let him out of your sight. I don't want this situation to get any messier than it is already. Understand?"

Etta promised.

Until that night, Etta hadn't considered that her father would even go near the Mason farm. But once she thought about it, she knew that it would only be a matter of time. The thought of what her father might do sent chills through her body.

She would do as the doctor had told her. She would watch her father . . . she would keep careful watch.

The chimes of the wall clock had never before sounded more lonely. Six o'clock. Etta slowly raised herself from the rocker. She picked up her suitcase and walked into the house, stopping only for one last, searching look down the wet, empty street.

"Hello, Jessie," Etta said into the phone. "This is Mrs. Pearson. Have you heard anything from Robert?"

"Why, no, Mrs. Pearson," Jessie answered. "I supposed he had come over to your house by now."

"No, he hasn't," Etta worried. "He was to be here

at three o'clock and it's after six now."

"Well, I'm sure he'll be there," Jessie replied, trying to reassure her. "He went down to get tires and he was going to have the brakes checked—you know, those things always take longer than you think. He'll be there, Mrs. Pearson. Don't you worry."

"I suppose you're right," Etta replied trying to believe it.

"Bob will probably be there any minute," Jessie repeated.

"Thank you," Etta said quietly.

She walked back to the window to watch for approaching cars. The rain splashed against their headlights. She hoped each car she saw would be Robert's. She waited for one to turn into her driveway, but the vehicles rolled straight past her house for other destinations. Finally, she stopped going to the window. She sat down in the overstuffed chair and listened to the cars passing...and to the sound of the rain.

"Where in the world could he be?" she wondered.

6

The sound of tires screeching to a stop against the pavement startled her. Etta heard the gravel scatter in her driveway and a car door slam shut several times.

"What on earth!" she wondered aloud.

Then, she heard someone yelling in her front yard and feet clubbing up the steps to her front porch.

"Ma!" she heard the voice call.

Etta hurried to look out the window just in time to see a man fall on the slippery wooden steps.

"Robert!" she gasped, as she opened the door. "Robert, are you all right?"

Her son pulled himself up against the banister and rolled his head to the side, attempting to focus his eyes on the open door. Leaning out from the railing, with rain streaking down his face, he tried to explain, "It was jes a li'l fall."

"Are you hurt?" Etta asked anxiously.

"Hell, no!" he snorted. "I'm not hurt—I hit on my ass!"

She reached out her hands to help, but he brushed by her, allowing the screen door to slam behind him. Inside, he stumbled over her waiting suitcase and sprawled out across the floor.

"What the hell was that!" he tried to figure out.

"What's the matter, Robert?" Etta questioned, but she knew the answer without asking. She had smelled that sickening, sweet odor too many times. She knew without seeing her son's relaxed, watery eyes.

"What's that dumb suitcase doing in front of the door?" he grumbled, trying to pull himself up.

"You told me to have it packed, remember?" she said. "Here, let he help you up."

Etta tried to take hold of his arm, but he pulled away from her, and staggered to his feet.

"Well, if you're ready, let's go," he shrugged.

His mother held her voice low, in forced natural tones. "We can't start with you like this."

He turned away from her, refusing to look her in the face. "Whatta ya mean, 'with me like this'?"

Still struggling to remain outwardly calm, she said, "Why, you're soaking wet—you'd catch your death of cold in those clothes."

His hands batted at the air as he slobbered through his words, "I told ya I was takin' ya to Osawatomie to see Uncle Theodore, and by damn, I'm gonna take ya there! So let's go!"

He reached for her suitcase, but Etta moved it aside.

"Robert, I'm not going with you in your condition," she said firmly.

He wrinkled his face and squinted his eyes, trying to see her clearly. "Why not?"

"Because you're drunk," she said flatly, tightening her words.

"I admit I had one drink," he fussed, "but that's nobody's business but mine."

"You've had more than *one* drink. You're drunk!" she repeated.

He shrugged his shoulders. "Suit yourself. Stay here if ya want, but I'm drivin' to Osawatomie to see poor Uncle Theodore. If ya don't want ta come, all right. I'll go without ya."

She planted herself firmly between him and the door. "You're not going anywhere!"

"Move outta my way!" he ordered whipping the air with his hands.

"I'm not moving anywhere and neither are you!" she replied determinedly. "You're too drunk to walk to the car, let alone drive. What do you want to do, kill yourself and someone else at the same time?

"Look at you!" she scolded. "You can't even stand up. You come in here stumbling around and slobbering all over yourself!"

Robert turned around, stamping his foot. "I'm not gonna hear you talk to me like that—jes like I was a kid!"

"Then grow up!" she demanded. "Grow up!"

He puckered his face. "Whatta ya want outta me?"

"I want you to be a man and act like a man. I want to be proud of you. Look at yourself—you look like a drowned rat! I've seen stray dogs look healthier—you're killin' yourself with drink!"

"So what!" he sniffed. "Who cares?"

She took hold of his shoulders. "I care!" she stressed, "and Jessie cares!"

He shook his head, slowly, and mumbled, "She'll leave me jes like the others did!"

Etta freed his shoulders and waved her hands helplessly in the air. "I wouldn't blame her if she did. Why would any woman want to stay with you, unless she wants to feed on your broken promises?... Promises...'I quit, Mom, I quit drinking,' you told me that only a week ago. 'This time I quit for good.' Hah! You make me sick with your broken promises. Lies! That's what they are—nothing but lies! How long can anyone put up with your lies? I'm sick of hearing them!"

Her voice toughened. "I called you this morning and said, 'Robert, I need you—I need you to help me.' Shouldn't a mother be able to say that to her son? I could have called the girls—Marguerite in Minnesota or Pauline in Seattle, and said, 'I need you,' and they would have come. But no, I called my son, right here in town, and said, 'I need your help. My brother's dying and I've got to go to him. I need your help!' Is that too much to ask? Is it?"

She didn't wait for an answer. "Why? Why can't
I ever count on you, Robert? Just once! I sat out there
on that porch for over three hours saying to myself,
'He'll come. He won't let me down this time. He
won't let me down.' But I knew better. Oh, God, I
knew. Your sense of responsibility slides under the first
saloon door you happen to see. Then, you come
wobbling out here like some dizzy animal, screaming
at the top of your voice, falling down and crawling
all over the front steps.

"You don't care!" she shouted. "You don't care
about anyone else but yourself! You don't care that
I've been waiting here, knowing my brother's dying
and I'm already half-sick with worry! You don't care!"

"Oh, Ma!" he cried and fell into her arms. "Don't
talk to me like that!" he coughed, drooling in his
tears. "You know I don't mean to—I can't help it,
Ma! I can't help it! I'm weak!"

His mother raised her arms and folded them around
him; her hand brought his head to rest in the curve
of her neck. "I know," her voice became gentle
as she caressed his head. "I know, son. It's not your
fault. It's in your blood—you can't help it. I love
you, son. I'll always love you."

"Oh, Ma," his voice choked, "I love you too."

"I know you do, Bobby, I know you do." She
kissed his face. "Now, let me take you into bed."

Holding on to him, his mother helped him through
the door. As he lay down, she guided his head to
the pillow, then raised his feet to rest on the covers.
She untied his shoes and removed them. Spreading

a quilt over him, she bent down and kissed his forehead.

"Good-night, Bobby," she said.

Marjorie, this is Aunt Etta," she spoke softly into the telephone. "I hoped that you would answer. I didn't want to talk to your mother. I want to talk to you."

"Aunt Etta," Marjorie was confused, "where are you? I thought you would be out of town by now. Where are you?"

"Shhh," Etta said. "I don't want your mother to hear."

"She can't—she and Daddy are upstairs. But where are you?"

"I'm home, Marjorie," Etta finally confessed.

"What's wrong, Aunt Etta?"

"Don't tell your mother. Robert's"... Etta hesitated... "Robert's intoxicated. I just put him to bed."

"Oh, no!"

"I'll tell you why I called," she said. "I phoned the train depot. There's a train leaving for Joplin at eight o'clock and I'm catching it. I want to know if you will go to Osawatomie with me?"

"I can't, Aunt Etta," the girl answered slowly.

"Now, your mother will let you if you ask her," Etta urged. "You're not in school. She's let you take the bus by yourself to visit Agnes. If you tell her you *want* to go with me, I know she'll let you."

"I can't, Aunt Etta, I just can't."

"Why, Marjorie?" Etta asked. "Why won't you go with me?"

"I can't," Marjorie repeated. "I just can't go up there with him dying and all. I just can't."

Etta took a deep breath. "All right."

"I'm sorry, Aunt Etta."

"That's all right, child. I understand," Etta told her. "But don't tell your mother I called."

"If you say so."

"Promise you won't tell her. I don't want her to know about Robert. When I get back, I'll tell her he was sick . . . or something. Now, promise?"

"I promise," Marjorie said.

Etta held her hand on the telephone for a moment, then she dialed another number. This call would bring a taxi. She was through with asking and arguing—of having her hopes built up and torn down. Etta's mind was clear. Her direction was settled. She had decided to take the eight o'clock train to Joplin, and from there, she would travel to Osawatomie. She would go alone.

"I'll do it myself," she said.

7

Etta fanned herself with a folded newspaper. The train had been late in arriving at the Springfield Station, delaying its departure past the scheduled time. During the long wait, the air in the coach had grown stale.

It was eight-thirty before Etta finally saw the depot pass by her window. Slowly, at first, the dingy blackened buildings that stood near the tracks moved by. Soon the streetlights were left behind as the train pulled out of town, heading due west toward Joplin, Missouri. At the Kansas border, the locomotive would veer northwest through Pittsburg, Fort Scott, and on to Etta's destination—Osawatomie.

Etta settled herself in the coach chair, leaning her head against the cushioned back, hoping to sleep.

But sleep would not come. Her eyes wouldn't close to the passing trees and the rolling hills, spotted with farmhouses.

Travel had always excited her. She had been six years of age when she journeyed from Indiana with her mother and father in a covered wagon. They had crossed the Mississippi River with their wagon lashed to a flatbed barge. Winding the rocky hills of Missouri in the horse-pulled wagon may have been just as dangerous, but a lone flatbed, guided by rope stretching across the giant river, seemed unnatural to her. Being surrounded by water had been a terrifying experience.

The Kansas Territory was opened in 1854, and three years later, shortly before the Civil War, the region became the thirty-fourth state. By 1888, when Etta and her parents emigrated to the area, the battle to be a free state had been won, and the bloody Civil War which had scarred the Kansas plains was twenty-three years in the past.

At the turn of the century, while settlers homesteaded in Kansas and Oklahoma, and Colorado and Utah, the coasts of two oceans had already been connected by railroad tracks and telegraph wires. In the East, a revolution of twentieth century industry was being introduced. The Wright Brothers had proven the possibility of flight. Edison had invented a moving picture and he had recorded, "Mary had a little lamb," on a wax cylinder. But all of these modern inventions were foreign to life in Kansas.

While New York City boasted of boardwalks and

elevated railways, wagon wheels were still etching paths across the grassy plains of Kansas. However, progress was on the move. By 1900, Kansas had more railroad tracks than any state in the Union, connecting its new towns by the racing steam engines.

Now, sitting in the moving train, Etta found herself mentally listing the ways she had traveled—covered wagon, flatbed boat, buckboard, sled, train and automobile. But she had never flown in an airplane. Often, she had watched the metallic crafts cut across the sky, holding her breath as if her doing so would help keep them aloft. Etta was convinced that flying was also an unnatural way for man to travel. Yet, she had crossed the Mississippi, and though she wouldn't confess it openly, she did sometimes long to ride in an airplane. Just the thought of it made her shiver.

Then, once again, the purpose of her journey came to mind, and her thoughts became engulfed in the past.

Where's Papa?" she asked as she walked toward the kitchen to refill the basin with cool water.

Agnes didn't know. And Dorothy had no idea. Both said that they thought he had gone upstairs to bed.

Etta looked in the bedroom—he wasn't there. There was no one on the porch either. As she walked back into the living room, she realized that something else was gone too. Etta stopped. Slowly, her eyes surveyed the room. The light from the kerosene lamp flickered, making moving shadows on the walls. Her attention was drawn to the stone fireplace. She then realized what was missing from the room—her father's shotgun had been removed from the wooden rack.

The new moon glowed round and full, spreading its silver light across the scorched prairies. The earth still radiated the heat it had amassed during the August day. Did she call after her father as she ran? She couldn't remember. She only knew that when she finally saw him, she began running even faster. She caught up with him at the gate of Parker Mason's farm.

Then she cried out to him, "Don't, Papa, please don't!"

She pulled at his shirt and tried to hold him back.

"Pa! Don't, Pa! Come back home. I'll do anything!" she pleaded with him. "Theodore will be all right, you'll see. I'll take good care of him, I promise! He'll be just fine. Papa, please come back with me! Theodore will be all right, I promise! Papa, listen to me!"

If her father heard her, he gave no indication. He walked straight toward Parker Mason's house, not stopping until he reached the front porch.

"Parker Mason!" he called. "Come out!"

Etta ran in front of her father and attempted to stand between him and the front door. He looked at her sharply, and she stepped aside, not knowing which way to turn or what to do.

"Parker Mason!" he called again. "Come out!"

Etta watched the door, praying that it was bolted and would not be opened. When she heard the latch move, her heart pounded. Then, she saw the door slowly open and Mrs. Mason stepped into the doorway, holding a kerosene lamp in her hand.

"What do you want?" Mrs. Mason's voice quivered. The woman didn't ask who had called for her husband—she knew the identity of the caller. Etta realized, even then, that Mrs. Mason had expected her father's visit.

"My business is with your husband, Mrs. Mason," her father said with stern resolve.

"He's not here," the woman replied shortly.

Etta's father's tone didn't change. "I don't believe you, Mrs. Mason."

"I tell you, he's not here!" she insisted.

Etta looked back at her father, hoping he would yield his stand, but he did not. "I'll not leave 'til I'm settled with him," he said.

Mrs. Mason stepped to the edge of the porch. She stood stiffly, looking down at Etta and her father. "Parker and me heard about the boy," she told them. "Believe me, we're terrible sorry. We ain't slept a night since we heard."

"Your husband can tell me that," Etta's father responded.

"I tell you, Parker meant no harm!" Mrs. Mason tried to convince him. "He only meant to scare the boy a little, so's he wouldn't come back. Parker never would've really hurt the boy. He didn't think the boy would take him so seriously. He only showed him the knife to scare him a little."

A gray cloud covered the moon, turning the night black as pitch. All that Etta could see was the light of the kerosene lamp reflecting Mrs. Mason's tired face. The three of them stood in silence as if waiting for the moon to return.

When finally the cloud had freed its captive, Etta's father spoke again.

"I'll not leave 'til your husband comes out to face me," he said.

"I tell you, he's almost out of his mind since he heard about the boy," Mrs. Mason repeated. "If you saw him, you'd know. He's gone half-mad with the thought of it. He's punished. I tell you, he's already punished enough. Please leave him be in his torment!"

"I'll determine that for myself," Etta's father told her.

Mrs. Mason stepped down from the porch, walked straight to Etta's father, and stopped directly in front of him. Holding the lamp between them, she looked squarely at her intruder. "You'll *talk* to him and nothing more?" she asked pointedly.

Looking into the woman's face, her father's voice became a whisper. "I promise," he said. "I will not kill your husband."

The woman held out her hand. "Then, you won't mind giving me that gun."

Her father handed the rifle to her. Etta took a deep breath. Her shaking legs almost crumpled in relief.

Finally, Mrs. Mason said, "I need your help. Parker is near out of his mind—he ain't et a bite or slept since he heard about your boy."

Now, the woman allowed herself to cry.

"He's been like he's in a cave," she said. "He won't talk to me. When I walk into a room where he is, he gets up and leaves. I tell you, we're both about crazy—me following him around and him opening that knife and closing it."

Her voice choked through the sobbing. "You've got to help me. I tell you, he didn't mean the boy no harm—I swear to God!" she cried.

"Where is your husband, Mrs. Mason?" Etta's father asked.

She held out the rifle, motioning toward the right of the house. "He went into the barn at lunchtime and bolted the door. He hasn't come out since. I've gone back and forth to the barn all day—knocking at the door, pleading with him to let me in. 'Go away!' he tells me. 'Go away!' He won't come out and he won't let me inside. I'm his wife and I love him and I worry about him, and he tells me to go away.

"Since dark," she continued, "all I've done is walk back and forth between the house and the barn. I tell you, I've cried and I've pleaded with him 'til I'm all cried out!"

"Maybe I can help," Etta's father said, trying to comfort the woman. "I'll do your husband no harm. Take me to him."

Etta followed the two of them around the side of the house and out toward the barn.

When they came to the building, her father called

out, "Mr. Mason, open the door. I want to talk with
you. I promised your wife I'd do you no harm and
I'm a man of my word."

They waited, but heard no reply.

Her father hit his fist on the door and called out
again, "Mr. Mason, open the door. Your wife is here
with me. I promised her I'd only talk to you. I'll
not harm you. Come out and we'll talk about this."

Etta turned to see a lone horse gallop across the
field, kicking its heels, scattering clouds of dust in the
moonlight. The gray horse whinnied and its screeching
sound echoed across the plains. The cows huddled
restlessly at the far corner of the fence, bellowing,
turning, bumping into each other.

"He even locked the animals out," Mrs. Mason
explained, frantically. Then she turned back to the
barn door, hitting her hands against the wood.
"Parker," she cried, "please, love, open the door!"

"Is the side door locked?" Etta's father wanted to
know.

Etta followed as her father and Mrs. Mason hurried
the length of the building. The door would not open.
Etta shivered as her father rammed his shoulder
against the barrier. He hit the door hard, then stepped
back and lunged again. Each time his shoulder
rammed the wood, it cracked and splintered, and
they could hear the latch weaken, metal scraping
against metal. With one final lunge, the door gave
way to her father's force. They stood before the opening
in silence.

Moonlight streaked the hayloft, its silver glow

slicing diagonal stripes through the darkness. As her father stepped into the barn, Etta and Mrs. Mason followed close behind. The light of the kerosene lamp searched the splintered walls and hidden corners for Parker Mason. Etta could not remember that a word had been spoken. And then, looking up, they saw him.

The knot was tied securely on the rafter hook. The rope was pulled taut by the weight it held. The noose closed tightly about the throat of Parker Mason. His arms and legs hung lifeless above the toppled ladder. Both of the man's ears had been severed from his head. His pearl-handled jackknife, spotted with dark stains, lay stilled on the ground.

Etta felt a hand urgently shaking her shoulder.

"Are you all right, ma'am?" she heard a voice say.

She looked up to see the conductor bending over her.

"Where am I?" she asked anxiously, suddenly realizing the answer.

"Are you all right?" he asked again. "Lady, when you screamed out, you woke up everyone in the car."

"Oh, I'm sorry," she said looking around, seeing the puzzled faces of the other passengers. "I was dreaming," she tried to explain.

"It sure must have been a bad one to make you scream out like that," the conductor said.

"Yes," Etta replied, "it was."

"Do you want a glass of water or anything?" he asked.

"No, I'll be all right," she said. "It won't happen again."

As the conductor walked away, Etta looked down at her watch—five minutes 'til nine. She raised her timepiece to her ear to see if it was still running. It was. She couldn't believe that the train had been moving less than thirty minutes. "How can one relive hours of memories in only minutes of reality?" she wondered.

She settled back in the seat and listened to the clicking sounds of the metal wheels clattering against the tracks.

"I'll stay awake," she told herself, "and try to think about something else." But she realized that asleep or awake, she wouldn't be able to control her thoughts.

Trains... what lonely things they are... especially at night... taking people away to other places, separating them from those they love. It was a train that had taken her away from Theodore. And Frank... Frank had taken her away from her brother too. And her father. It was as if the three of them—Frank, her father and the train—had plotted against her.

When Frank heard about Theodore, he took off from work to come to Etta. During his visit, they would sit on the porch where she could listen for her brother's call. She and Frank must have talked, but the memory of what may have been said was gone. She only remembered that Frank was there and he had been a comfort to her.

"Do you love Frank?" her father asked directly.

"Yes," she had to answer.

"Then marry him."

"I will," she said, "as soon as Theodore is well."

"Marry him now," her father told her.

"I can't—not now," Etta objected. "Not with Theodore the way he is."

The stroke had left the boy unable to care for himself. Theodore had become completely dependent upon her. Words were impossible for him to form. And his thick-tongued sounds were distinguishable only to Etta. The boy didn't even try to communicate with anyone except his sister. Her father was aware of this.

Etta's father was a stern man, but his appearance was never more commanding than when he was seated in the highbacked rocker. Etta would go to any length not to displease her father, nor would she have dreamed of questioning his authority, especially when he was seated in his rocker.

"Your brother is not going to get better," her father said, bluntly. "He has lost his chance for life. I will not let you give him yours. You marry Frank."

"All right," Etta said. "Agnes will be through grade school this spring. I'll marry him then."

"I don't want you to wait until spring. You marry him now."

Finally, she agreed.

That was all that had been said. It was settled. In three weeks, she and Frank Pearson were married.

Etta remembered waving good-bye to her family as

she and Frank boarded the train for Topeka. Her father's wave was abrupt. . . almost matter-of-fact. Her mother's good-bye was a lingering embrace. Her sisters were excited—Dot and Agnes jumped and ran the length of the wooden depot platform. But it was Theodore's good-bye that Etta could never forget, for it was no good-bye at all. The young boy stood on the platform and silently watched his sister leave.

And ten years later. . . ten years later it had been by train that she had taken her brother to the State Hospital for the Mentally Ill.

"The boy can't stay here any longer," Frank told her. "He is nineteen and no better than he was ten years ago. He's like a three-year-old and he always will be. There is no life for him here."

The boy had grown to the height of a man, but in his actions he remained a child. Words were still difficult for him to form and placing three words in order with any spontaneity was next to impossible. His mouth was held half-open, and his eyes appeared startled, as they constantly searched his surroundings with the quick, darting, movement of a trapped animal.

Theodore enjoyed the games of young children, but even the younger ones soon became bored with his inability to play with any skill. It was impossible for him to catch a ball, and after the humor of his groping and stumbling passed, the children would either ignore him or they would delight in teasing him. Being ignored frustrated and angered him, while teasing often made him laugh, for he revelled in the attention. When pushed into anger, he would strike out as any three-year-old, slapping at the others. Theodore had no concept of his own strength. It was because of his physical power that Frank saw the boy as a potential threat to his own children and to the neighborhood youngsters as well.

"I can take care of Theodore!" Etta said shortly.

"I won't let you make a pet of him," Frank said bluntly. "I won't stand for it! It's not fair to you and it's not fair to our children. Etta, you must think of the children. Robert has started to school. Little Pauline will start next fall and Marguerite will begin the year after. They're young now and they love having Theodore here. But that won't last. Soon the other children will make comments about him and they'll grow to be ashamed of him. The women in the church make excuses for not coming here now."

"I don't care about the church women!" Etta said in defense.

"You must care," he reasoned, "if not for yourself, you must care for the children. We don't want them to grow up in a house that is avoided by the neighbors. We must think of their futures. At the State Hospital they will take good care of Theodore."

"But will they love him?" Etta asked.

Frank ignored her question. "He'll be with others like himself. There, he'll be respected for what he can do."

"Give me more time to think about it?" her voice was pleading. "Let me talk to Dot and Agnes again. I know I can make them understand!"

"They understand now, Etta," he said. "They don't want Theodore, even for a day. Since your mother died, neither one of them has come to the house, and they won't as long as he's here."

"Give me just another month," she said in desperation.

Her husband pulled an envelope from his coat pocket and slipped the folded papers from the enclosure. "On my way home from Kansas City, I stopped at Osawatomie. The arrangements are made. There is space available for your brother now."

Etta took the papers and slowly read the forms. She then sat silently.

"I got another letter from my brother, Tom, in Springfield, Missouri," her husband spoke again. "There is a boom of building there. The government is building a new prison hospital. They need bricklayers and the wages are high."

"How long will you be gone this time?" she wondered aloud, still looking at the papers in her hand.

"I plan to take you and the children with me. We can stay with Tom and Alice until we find a house. Tom says there's no end to the construction there.

"Don't you see? We have to find a place for Theodore now," he said, leaning forward. "If we took him to Missouri, we would have to wait a year to be considered residents before we could apply at the State Hospital there. We must put him in the sanitarium now. Then, we can move to Missouri and start our lives anew. All of this will be left behind us."

Her husband waited for her answer, not wanting to rush her, for he knew that logic was to his advantage. Finally, Etta complied. She agreed to take

Theodore to the State Hospital at Osawatomie.

"Why?" Etta wondered, as she leaned her head against the coach chair. "Why do the years fade away but their memories remain so fresh...so clear?"

Finally, Etta's eyelids grew heavy and closed, but in her sleep, her mind would not allow her rest—the dream she had the night before returned. She saw herself standing in an open field, the vermillion sun circling a black, watery sky. Shadows moved across the grassy plains, stopping only briefly to notice her. She started to follow them, but a large iron gate barred her passing. Each time she turned, another locked gate stood before her. She looked through the steel bars and watched the spectral figures pass on the other side.

"Etta," a voice called to her. Turning from one gate to another, she searched. Who had called? She wanted to know. The surrounding figures would not answer. Instead, they slowly raised their hands and waved to her. Then, they drifted away...all but one...one distant form remained, standing alone...watching her from the silent, dusty road. Etta pressed her face against the metal gate that separated them.

"Etta," the voice called once more. Then the boy turned and walked down the quiet road.

"Theodore!" she cried out. "Wait for me!"

Etta sat up straight, finding herself trembling. The shriek of the train whistle tore at her ears. She pulled a handkerchief from her handbag and blotted beads of perspiration from her face.

"Next stop, Joplin!" the conductor called.

8

It was ten o'clock when Dr. Ivan Watts completed his speech to the Ladies' Auxiliary of the First Baptist Church of Osawatomie, Kansas. The speech had been the success he expected since he had frequently presented it to other groups.

In a town the size of Osawatomie, guest speakers were not easily come by, other than ministers of churches and the high school principal. Dr. Watts was a man of respected intellect. His appearance was enhanced by thick, steel-gray hair which fell casually across his forehead, almost touching his ragged black brows. His startling brown eyes were direct and in constant motion.

Osawatomie women had long before agreed that Dr. Watts was, indeed, a handsome man. The fact that he had become a widower three years previously added to his charming personality. Even though most of the women in the group were married, it didn't discourage their admiration for the director of the Kansas State Hospital for the Mentally Ill.

Although his talk had become standardized over the eight years he had been on the staff, he patiently repeated it. He realized that it was groups such as these that furnished the major portion of volunteer services at the hospital. And although he somewhat resented having to "go begging" for these volunteers and playing politics to raise needed funds, he had to admit he enjoyed speaking to groups.

His walk had been brisk as he entered the small auditorium and took his place at the lectern. He thoroughly relished those first moments before a group—standing alone, looking down at flowered hats and neatly crossed legs. It was his custom to wait until the flowered hats tilted upward, revealing the faces beneath. He made a point of looking into each pair of eyes, individually, and never commenced speaking until total silence filled the room.

"When visitors come to the hospital," he began by letting the volume of his voice fill the room, "I often notice them whispering to each other, wondering if I am one of the doctors or one of the patients. If they don't ask which I am, I always extend them the same courtesy—I don't ask *them* if they are visitors or patients."

Chuckles filled the small meeting room.

"I don't know of any of our doctors," he continued,

"who would mind being mistaken for patients, but there are many patients who would take it as a personal affront if they were mistaken for doctors."

Now the ladies laughed and Dr. Watts felt that his first objective of relaxing his audience was achieved.

As the laughter faded, the doctor's face grew serious. "Why do we have a state hospital for the mentally ill?" he asked, thoughtfully directing the question to himself. "Because," he answered, "mental illness strikes all ages and all income brackets."

Ivan Watts had a thorough respect for history because he never considered it to be a list of dates and places, but the result of human conditions. He felt people should be reminded that mental illness had not been introduced by the pressures of the twentieth century, but that neuroses, psychoses, and brain injury had plagued mankind long before bearded men in Vienna began inventing terminologies.

And he enjoyed telling the story of the inception and evolution of the State Hospital. The buildings and the facilities hadn't suddenly sprouted and grown at the edge of town. The development of the Kansas State Hospital for the Mentally Ill had been launched over a century before.

The site for the hospital was determined as a result of several history-making coincidences. Late in 1854, the Reverend Samuel Lyle Adair, college trained and an ordained minister of the Congregational Church, brought his family from Ohio to settle in the infant village of Osawatomie. He planned to establish a church there among the small collection of settlers.

His wife, the former Florella Brown, had a brother who shared her husband's views in the opposition of slavery. Her brother's name was plain and unimposing, but one that would soon strike terror across the Territory of Kansas—*John Brown.*

Following his sons and their families to Osawatomie, the elder John Brown brought with him a generous supply of guns and ammunition. All of the Territory of Kansas was divided in the struggle to determine whether or not Kansas would be a slave or free state. John Brown's views were in no way divided—at all costs, even death, he was a dedicated abolitionist. The year after his arrival in Osawatomie proved to be fired with turbulence for the settlers in this region.

In May, 1856, John Brown's oldest son, John, Jr., led a local group of men toward Lawrence, Kansas, intending to protect the Free State town from a threatened invasion. However, before Brown's militia reached their destination, they received news that Lawrence had already fallen, so they made camp to await further instructions.

During the delay, the restless and radical John Brown, leading a small group of men, advanced to the pro-slavery settlement at the Dutch Henry Crossing of the Marais des Cygnes River. While there, five defenseless pro-slavery settlers were murdered. There is little doubt that Brown and his four comrades were responsible.

Although at the beginning, John, Jr.'s, zeal matched his father's, when the young man heard about the brutality of the massacre he became disturbed. The incident weighed heavily on his conscience. Within days, he lapsed into a state of acute melancholy and was relieved of his command. When the young man returned to his family, his condition had worsened to the point that he did not recognize his wife or friends.

The armed conflict in the region and the murderous acts of John Brown's men caused pro-slavery forces to direct their attention toward Osawatomie. The small town of anti-slavery settlers was an outpost penetrating deeply into pro-slavery territory.

The heat of August brought with it the fire of battle. On August 30, a large pro-slavery force attacked the small town. Although the bands of men led by Brown and Dr. W. W. Updegraff fought defiantly, they were severely outnumbered and forced to retreat. Most of the homes and buildings were put to the torch, and the countryside was blackened with destruction.

As the tide of the struggle turned toward the side of anti-slavery, those individuals and communities that had most actively supported the Free State cause automatically gained statewide prestige and power. The Battle of Osawatomie had been significant. The town became the choice site for the 1859 convention for the establishment of the Republican Party of Kansas. Horace Greeley, a national figure, demonstrated his admiration for the community by speaking favorably of it at the convention.

The governor of Kansas delivered his message to the legislature in January of 1863, referring to the portion of the state constitution which encouraged the establishment of institutions for the insane. "This appeal is directed to you. The state which cares best for those unfortunates is always the truest in council and the noblest in action," he said.

On January 16, 1863, only a few days after Abraham Lincoln signed the Emancipation Proclamation, a bill was introduced in the Kansas House of Representatives for the location of the state insane asylum. Wyandotte and Paola were among the towns considered as prospective sites, but due to its decisive record of opposition to slavery, the remote town of Osawatomie received the vote of the lawmakers.

"In the two years following, the state of Kansas was literally bathed in blood," Dr. Watts delighted in emphasizing. His voice always deepened with his reference to blood when speaking to women to produce their expected reactions. If their moans were sufficient, he would proceed—if not, he had alternative scenes of gore to describe.

"During the Civil War, more men met death in battle in our state than in any other state in the Union," he would say, dramatically. "In 1865, the War Between the States came to an end. Now, the legislature could turn its attention toward the rapidly growing population and the problems that large numbers of people ultimately bring."

Across the wooded banks of the Marais des Cygnes River, a mile northeast of the main part of Osawatomie, the terrain rises in a long, low ridge. This was the site chosen for the state insane asylum.

"In 1866, a Quaker physician, Dr. C. O. Gause,

came to Osawatomie with his wife, Levisa, and their infant daughter. Dr. Gause was the first superintendent of the facilities, such as they were. Entries in his journal indicate that Dr. Gause was sympathetic and humane in his treatment of patients. He strongly objected to the manner in which many patients were brought to the farmhouse structure, built to house both the family of the superintendent, and the patients.

"'The seventh patient,' Dr. Gause wrote in his journal, 'was brought here in a wagon, tied hand and foot. She had been hauled miles, in cold weather, in this condition, from her home which was over one hundred miles distance. Deception was used in bringing this patient to the asylum which is a great detriment to her. She has been kept at home under close confinement in a house built for this purpose, and from which she effected her escape a number of times.'

"As Matron, Mrs. Gause fulfilled her duties with dedicated vigor and loving-kindness. One of the entries in the journal tells of her pursuit after an escaped patient through three cornfields before she could persuade him to return to the hospital."

Dr. Watts raised his bushy brows suggestively. "Of course, women have been known to chase a man over more rugged terrain with other motives in mind." His face then broke into a large grin to share the amusement with the ladies... and they loved it!

After the hospital admitted its first patient, two decades of Indian raids remained to be endured. The railroad had not yet reached Dodge City. Bat Masterson was a young boy—only twelve years old—

and enormous herds of buffalo roamed the western half of the state. The economic level of the state had sunk to its lowest depths. Over thirty thousand would-be settlers abandoned their land and moved east. Personal indebtedness was widespread, for there was drought and depression.

"Against this background of hardships, the fact that Kansas had a sense of responsibility for its unfortunate mentally ill became even more noble, I believe," Dr. Watts told the audience.

"Construction on the 'Old Main' building began in 1868. The rambling red brick structure was raised to five stories. It is the oldest and largest mental hospital building in the state. The two towers, which give it a castle-like appearance, have become a landmark.

"Sadly, it was built at a time when the concept toward the mentally ill was, 'isolation,'" said Dr. Watts. "Today, this concept is changing. The hospital's goal now is to be a part of the community. Every day we discover new ways to use the talents of our employees and volunteers from our community to help in the patient's rehabilitation and well-being.

"Now, we are engaged in bringing the community to the patient and, most importantly, bringing the patient back into the community. Through the use of new drugs, treatment programs, and closer cooperation between the hospital and local social welfare agencies, nearly three thousand mentally ill persons are receiving treatment. The periods of patient internment are becoming shorter—approximately 50 percent return home within six months, and 85 percent in twelve months."

Now, Ivan Watts leaned forward, resting his elbow on the podium. His tone of voice became lower. . . more personal.

"At one time," he said softly, "Londoners who were willing to pay a penny were allowed to wander through the crowded wards of Bedlam Hospital for a Sunday afternoon's entertainment. The shrieks and groans and unusual behavior of the patients were a source of amusement and diversion in a more callous age.

"Fifty years ago, on a warm Sunday afternoon," he said, "the curious walked up 'Asylum Hill' at Osawatomie to watch the patients who were brought outside and placed in a fenced enclosure. Groups of adults and children walked around the caged victims much as we might tour a zoo today.

"No more!" he said, standing up straight. "Today, groups of adults and children come to the hospital, not to *be* entertained but to entertain the patients. They invite patients into their homes to share Sunday dinner. They take them to church, to concerts, and to social and civic events. Today, the State Hospital, at last, has become a part of *your* community because you are willing to become a part of *our* community.

"You may rightfully feel a sense of pride in the accomplishments of your state's mental health program, for you have taken an active part in its advancement. In the last two decades, we have brought Kansas from forty-seventh among forty-eight states to first place in the nation in its mental health facilities and treatment."

The speaker walked around the lectern to stand in front of it. He now looked into the faces under the flowered hats.

"Will the next hundred years repeat the progression-regression-progression cycle? Or, will Kansas marshal the forces of research, education and training to hold and increase the gains it has made in the under-standing and acceptance of the mentally ill, and in the treatment of mental illness—the number one major health problem of the world?"

He raised his open hands. "The decision, ladies, rests in this room."

Since Dr. Watts was accustomed to a standing ovation, the look of surprise that crossed his face was political, not emotional. Before leaving the small church auditorium, he received what he had come after—a promise from the Ladies' Auxiliary of the First Baptist Church to adopt a ward of twelve people at the hospital, and to be responsible for birthday parties and special trips for those patients.

After consuming his share of refreshments and receiving more compliments than his ego required, Dr. Watts left the church. He had intended to drive straight home, but at the last corner before his street, he changed directions. His car followed the narrow strip of paved highway to the rusty metal bridge crossing the winding Marais des Cygnes River, then drove up the road leading to the main building of the State Mental Hospital. This was his usual nightly trip. How many nights since Emily's death had he started home only to turn away at the last minute? He didn't know—he had lost count. He only knew that there was nothing now to draw him to the lonely house. So, once again, he drove to the towering brick building to substitute the problems of others for his own.

9

Only the desk lamp glowed in the darkened room as Ivan Watts returned to his office that night. His key unlocked the door allowing the lights from the hallway to flash briefly across the tiled floor. In the night hours, he never used the overhead lights— he enjoyed the silent darkness around him. Often, he would sit at his desk and lean back in his swivel chair to smoke a cigarette and drink a cup of black coffee that he had picked up at the commissary. Here, alone in his office, the doctor tried to clear his thoughts.

The opened telegram lay on the corner of the mahogany desk. Nearby rested a file, measuring over three inches thick, of papers recording nearly forty years of medical data, clinical reports and correspondence pertaining to one patient, a testimony that a man named Theodore Morrison did exist.

He had hardly settled himself in his chair, and hadn't taken the time to taste the coffee, when the yellow piece of paper caught his attention. His hand reached out and drew the paper toward him. He leaned forward to reread the message which concluded:

"Will be there soon as possible—Mrs. Frank Pearson."

Reaching for the thick brown folder, he centered it before him and turned back the cover. He began thumbing through the voluminous sheets that varied in color due to aging. The yellowed entrance forms, dated July 23, 1913, stated:

Patient Admitted: Theodore Morrison
Sex: Male
Race: White
Born: May 6, 1894
Age: Nineteen years, two months
Height: Five feet, six inches
Weight: 130 Pounds
Color of Hair: Light Brown
Color of Eyes: Blue
Identifying Marks: Diagonal scar, left checkbone
Parent or Guardian: Mrs. Frank Pearson, sister

The initial examination of Theodore Morrison concluded: "Mentally incompetent due to severe sunstroke or strokes. Patient's assigned number: 13784."

The name, Theodore Morrison, was absent from subsequent reports and examination sheets. The number, 13784, was stamped in its place. Incoming and outgoing correspondence with his sister, Mrs. Pearson, all had the number, either stamped or written, in the corners for proper identification in filing.

Turning the pages, brief statements caught Dr. Watts' attention:

October 10, 1923—this patient's behavior is uniform. He is quiet, orderly and occupies himself with simple ward duties—is very easily excited, and at infrequent intervals becomes disturbed for short periods. His usual behavior, however, is agreeable. He is communicative and jocular. Enjoys excellent health, eats well, sleeps well, attends and enjoys all entertainments provided for patients and appears to be entirely satisfied with present residence.

The doctor came across many letters written by Mrs. Pearson relating her concern for her brother's health and happiness. Each one accounted that she had sent five dollars or so for the purchasing of "something special" for her brother. Stapled to these letters were replies from the head nurse or administrating doctor. On May 7, 1942, one letter read:

Yes, Mrs. Pearson, Mr. Morrison knows who is sending him the gifts and frequently enjoys showing his new shoes and bathrobe to other patients and staff members.

March 7, 1947, another letter to Mrs. Pearson stated:

We asked Mr. Morrison what he would like to buy with the two dollars you sent. As you know, he loves candy, and his answer was, of course, "candy." For that reason, we decided to buy him candy, periodically, which he will enjoy more than anything else.

Leafing through further pages, Dr. Watts came to his first entry in the crowded file. The number, 13784, had disappeared from the heading at his insistence and all patients since the beginning of his administration were identified by name. He read the comments:

September 8, 1948: Patient, Theodore Morrison, age 46. Mr. Morrison is delusional at times and confused. However, he is able to converse and state his desires. The only medication he receives is Vitamin B Complex. He seems happy in present state. His greatest pleasure is smoking his pipe. His sister sends him various things he needs. He is not able to walk due to recently fractured hip.

Then Dr. Watts noticed the first letter that he, himself, had received from Mrs. Pearson:

Dear New Doctor—the one who takes care of my brother—Theodore Morrison—I don't have your name:

I am concerned about my brother. I read in the newspaper where several patients had died from the heat. It is raining here in Springfield, and much cooler. I hope it is raining there and much cooler, too.

I wish I could see Theodore. I believe it would make him feel better and me ditto. Maybe I will get a chance to come see him soon.

It was that same year, Dr. Watts remembered, that he first saw Mrs. Pearson. He would never forget that meeting. She had marched straight into his office and announced, "I am here to take my brother home with me!"

"Don't you think we should discuss this, Mrs. Pearson?" he remembered asking.

"Now, don't you start arguing with me," she scolded. "My whole family's done nothing but fuss with me about it. Anyway, I'm in no mood to argue anymore. I've made up my mind!"

She stood unmoving before him, looking straight into his eyes.

He remembered that he had tried to appear as casual as possible. "Mrs. Pearson," he said softly, "I just think it might be wise if we discussed it."

"That's what my sisters say, too," she replied. "'Discuss it.' But what they really mean is *argue.* What do you mean when you say, 'discuss'?" she asked bluntly.

"I mean, talk it over," he answered. "Won't you please sit down?"

"I'm not tired," she said stubbornly. "I can talk standing up. I don't intend to be here long."

"But, I'm a little tired," he told her. "If you stand, I'll have to stand too. Won't you please sit down?"

Reconsidering the offer, Etta Pearson sat down.

However, she did not lean back in the padded leather chair, but seated herself erectly, as if a poker had been stuffed in her corset.

Dr. Watts could vividly recall the attitude—the sound of her words, even the sternness in her posture—but he couldn't remember her face. Perhaps it had blended and faded with those of numerous patients' relatives he'd encountered. But he could still see her eyes—cold, blue eyes, open and honest in their directness. Yes, he remembered Mrs. Pearson's eyes stubbornly defying him to oppose her.

"Mrs. Pearson," he recalled telling her, "if you want to take your brother home with you, I won't stop you."

"Good!" she said abruptly.

"However, I think there are several things you need to consider."

"I've thought it all out," she interrupted. "As you know, I am a widow now. All my children are away from home and I live alone. I have plenty of room. I can take care of Theodore, and I would give him a lot of attention."

"I'm sure you would," the doctor said, "but it's because you live alone that I think you should reconsider such an action carefully. As you know, since Mr. Morrison's fall, he has great difficulty in walking. He would have to have a wheelchair. He would require help in getting up and down stairs, and in and out of bed. This is hardly a job for a woman of your age. How old are you, Mrs. Pearson?"

Her body stiffened. "I hardly think that is any of your business!"

Even now, Dr. Watts shuddered when recalling the tone of her answer. He knew that he had chosen the wrong question.

"I mean," he said trying to backtrack, "this is not a proper job for any woman of any age."

"I'm a strong woman, Dr. Watts," she said flatly. "I'm strong enough to do anything I set my mind to!"

"I bet you are," he found himself agreeing, "but I'd like for you to think it over again. Your brother has been in this hospital nearly forty years. This has become his home."

"His *home* is with me," she argued, "where he can be cared for and loved."

"Mr. Morrison is loved here. Perhaps not as you would love him, but here, he has friends and companionship, and a routine that he is accustomed to. It could be very serious for him to be taken away— away from those he knows and the surroundings that he's familiar with. You see, Mrs. Pearson, the staff and the residents here have become Mr. Morrison's family."

"But they're not flesh and blood," she snapped.

"No," he agreed, "we're an adopted family. But still, we are the family your brother has learned to respect and depend upon. Mrs. Pearson, Theodore's only concern is for today. For him, there is no yesterday and there is no tomorrow—only today. He isn't aware of his past and the future has no meaning to him. Life, for him, is now. His reactions are controlled by habit, not memory."

"He remembers me," she said, desperately. "He

knows me!"

The doctor didn't attempt an answer. "I don't mean to be personal about your affairs, Mrs. Pearson, but during the last year, your brother has been in a hospital ward three times. During one admittance, he stayed over a month. Do you realize what costs you might incur for such a period in a private hospital?"

"The good Lord will provide," she said resolutely.

"Perhaps He already has, Mrs. Pearson," Dr. Watts said, quietly. "He has provided a home for your brother here."

The old woman turned her head away and sat in silence as the doctor spoke patiently to her.

"If you take Theodore now," Dr. Watts continued, "you would be taking him out of the state of Kansas. If, sometime later, you needed our services, it would make his return here impossible. That would mean you would have to seek aid in Missouri. Such assistance might not be readily available. Are you sure you want to take such a chance?"

"My daughter is waiting for me outside," she said, refusing to answer the question. "I want to see my brother now."

She stood up and Dr. Watts followed her to the door.

"Will you think over what I've said?" he said, kindly.

Her eyes were piercing in defiance; however, she nodded her head abruptly, then turned and walked down the hall.

It was afternoon when Etta Pearson returned to Dr. Watts' office.

"I've thought over what you said to me this morning," she told him. "I was with my brother for over an hour. Oh, Dr. Watts, it was almost as if I wasn't there at all. We sat outside on the yard benches in the shade, and he hardly listened to a word I said. Some of the other patients stood inside the door, looking out, and Theodore kept saying, 'I better go back in—they're waiting for me.'"

She took a deep breath. "I tried to talk to him about going home with me, but he wouldn't listen. He doesn't want to go home with me," she said. "You were right—this is his home and I'm simply a visitor who comes to force myself into his life. My heart tells me to take Theodore home and care for him. . .he'd be where I could see him and I wouldn't have to wonder about how he is or what he's doing. . .but my mind tells me to leave him here.

"It seems like all my life, people have told me to leave Theodore alone," she said. "First, my father. . . then, my husband. . .my sisters. . .now you. All right. I'll give in."

"I think you've made the best choice, Mrs. Pearson," he said quietly. "Your brother is, indeed, a lucky patient, for he has someone who loves him and is concerned. Many of our patients are forgotten people. But Mr. Morrison isn't forgotten because he has you."

Suddenly, Mrs. Pearson stood up. "Well, my sisters will be glad about this," she said. "What will I tell them?" she wondered aloud.

"Why tell them anything?"

One side of Etta's mouth pulled into a sly grin.

"You're a man with good ideas. It's none of their business, is it?"

They both laughed.

The letter he found in the folder came a short time after their visit. It was addressed to him:

> *Dear Dr. Watts:*
>
> *I hope we are friends. I have thought about nothing but what you said to me since I got home. I still worry about Theodore. I can't help it. I wonder about him so much. But I know there isn't anything I can do for him. That is what hurts me. How I would love to see him every day. I say grace every meal. I eat and ask Jesus to bless Theodore and those who are so good to him. I wish I could visit him more often and talk to him. But it is not possible. Please tell him, Etta loves him (that is what he calls me). I am sending him five dollars. Please buy him something he likes. Thank you and may God bless my little brother and all of you.*

Dr. Watts briskly turned the remainder of pages to the latest medical report on patient Theodore Morrison, which stated that he had again been admitted in the Carmichael Building "suffering a urinary infection and intensified respiratory complications which have developed into bilateral pneumonia."

Dr. Watts placed Etta Pearson's telegram between the pages and closed the bulky folder. Three and one-half inches of yellowing paper contained in a worn, brown folder—hardly a fitting account for fifty-nine years of a man's life, he thought.

Although the coffee was now cold, Ivan Watts finished drinking it. He walked across to the leather divan and stretched out, placing a cushion beneath his head. At last, he was exhausted. Now, sleep would come.

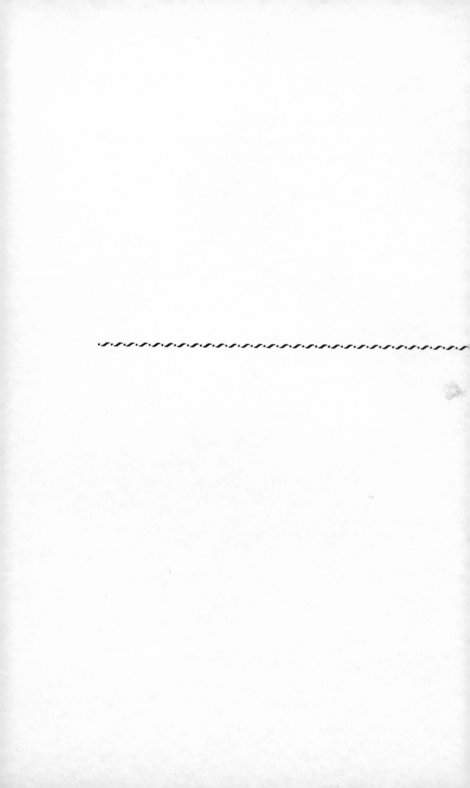

August 14, 1953

10

In the early morning hours, Ivan Watts was awakened by the sound of his office door closing. He sat up abruptly and looked around the room. Ten minutes until six, his watch indicated. His hands rubbed feeling into his face and sleep from his eyes. Then he noticed that a worn, black suitcase had been placed close to his desk. His eyes once more searched the room.

At that moment, his office door opened again and a round, gray-headed woman entered the room carrying a tray.

"Good morning," she said.

"Who are you?" he asked, then realized the identity of his visitor before she answered.

"Etta Pearson," she replied, walking toward his

desk. "I have some orange juice and black coffee. The lady in the cafeteria said she'll let us know when the eggs and bacon are ready."

"I never eat breakfast," he said, gruffly.

"That's what she told me, Doctor," Etta answered. "I asked her to prepare it anyway. Now, why don't you drink your juice and coffee. By the time you shave and change your clothes, breakfast will be here."

He automatically accepted the glass of juice she handed him and emptied its contents in three quick swallows.

"Well, you won't lose any of the vitamins gulping it like that," she commented.

"Now, your coffee," she said, handing him the cup. "I took the liberty of getting a cup for myself. I hope you don't mind."

"Oh, of course not," he replied with sarcasm edging his voice. "Make yourself right at home. Feel free to order some breakfast for yourself too, if you like."

"I did," she said, sitting down at the far side of the room to drink her coffee. "We can have breakfast together. The coffee is very good," she commented. "I think, on trains, they have recipes for the world's worst coffee—I could hardly drink the stuff."

Dr. Watts drank his coffee without saying a word. When he finished, he placed the cup on the floor by the leg of the couch, then stood up to walk into the adjoining bathroom.

"If you'll hand out your wrinkled suit," Etta instructed, "I'll put it on a hanger."

The tone of Ivan Watts' voice revealed his annoyance. "I don't think that's necessary!"

"Do you intend to put it on a hanger yourself?" she inquired.

"I do not!" he replied.

"I didn't think so," she said, "so, you hand it to me and I will."

He stopped at the door of the bathroom, looking at her directly. His visitor's eyes met his—they were the eyes he remembered from their previous meeting.

"You'd better get a move on," she prodded. "Our breakfast will be here any minute."

He was in no mood to start off his day by arguing with an invading old woman, but he slammed the door to display the extent of his annoyance.

After he had showered and shaved, he rememberd that his clean suit was in the closet on the other side of his office. Slowly, he cracked the door to peek out to see if his guest had mercifully vanished. She hadn't. She was still waiting. Her arm reached across the opening, holding the clean suit in her hand.

"Hand your wrinkled suit out to me and I'll give you this one," she ordered. "Pants first!"

"Mrs. Pearson, really!" he exclaimed.

"Do as I tell you!" she demanded. "Why, you'd look right silly trotting out here in your shorts. By the way, do you have clean shorts in there!"

His voice was exhausted. "Well, I never!"

"Do you or don't you?" she interrupted.

"Yes, I do!" he replied in exasperation.

"Good!" Etta said. "Now, hand me your trousers."

Ivan Watts did as he was ordered.

"Now, the coat. Thank you."

His pressed suit was held up to the door. He reached out and whisked it inside, slamming the door again.

Having dressed. Dr. Watts adjusted the knot of his striped tie and ran the comb through his hair, letting the usual front strands fall casually across his forehead.

When, at last, he opened the door, Etta announced, "Breakfast is served."

"I assure you, Mrs. Pearson," he said, standing in the doorway, "I make out quite nicely without such help."

She looked over at the rumpled divan. "So I noticed," she said.

There was a nervous briskness in Dr. Watts' step as he walked across to his chair. A plate of eggs, bacon and toast awaited the reluctant man. His cup had been refilled with steaming black coffee.

"I never eat breakfast," he repeated.

"Breakfast is the most necessary meal to the human body," Etta quoted, mechanically. "Isn't that what you tell your patients?"

He refused to answer.

Etta pointed at his plate. "Physician, heal thyself!" she said.

Dr. Watts briefly considered how the headlines might read—"Doctor at Mental Hospital Throws Old Woman Out of Window."

He picked up a slice of toast and declared, "I'll eat this."

His toast hardly touched his lips when his hand

stopped, frozen by the old woman's voice.

"Our Father," she began with her head bowed, "we thank you for this food. May it nourish our bodies as your love nourishes our souls. We ask that Jesus give Theodore special care at this time and strength to those who wait his hour. Thank you for helping me be, once again, with my good friend, Dr. Watts. I ask that you bless his useful life. Amen."

The doctor bit slowly into the piece of toast and within a short time, his plate of eggs and bacon had been scraped clean.

At last, Etta Pearson spoke again. "Well, I feel better. Breakfast always makes the world look brighter."

"I'm afraid I have to agree with you," he smiled.

They sat quietly, finishing their coffee.

"Are you married?" Etta asked abruptly.

"I was," he replied.

"Divorced?"

"No, I'm a widower."

"Sorry to hear that," she said. "How long?"

"What?"

"How long have you been a widower?"

"Three years."

"That's a long time for a man," she considered aloud.

"Why don't you marry again?" Etta asked unabashed. Without waiting for an answer, she pursued the subject. "You're still a young man. What? Forty-five? And a young forty-five, I might add. But you're not going to be young much longer if you continue catching catnaps on that sofa."

The doctor felt he had been attacked again. "Well, I don't think. . ."

"We often don't, until it's too late," she interrupted. "The only advantage in becoming old is that you can say exactly what you think. Take me, for instance. I have just inquired into your personal life and you don't like it, but you're thinking—'If I'm rude to the old woman and she should die on the way home, I'd never forgive myself.' Right? Of course it is. So people tolerate me and answer my questions. It may be that I use my advantage too often, but I learn an awful lot that way."

They both laughed.

"Now," she persisted, refusing to let the subject drop, "why haven't you remarried?"

"I suppose," he offered meekly, "I haven't met anyone I want to share my life with."

"Have you looked?" she inquired.

"No," Dr. Watts admitted.

"Well, then it's time you started looking," she told him. "Start now, before you have to settle for someone old and wrinkled like me."

"I'm sure I could do worse," he replied with a smile.

"I'm sure you could, but that's life," she mused.

She placed her cup on the corner of his desk. "Now," she said, "I'd better see Theodore. He's waiting for me."

"I'll go upstairs with you, if you like," Dr. Watts said, standing up.

She turned toward him. "That's why I came here first. You see, I'm a woman who likes to have the strength of a man nearby at a time like this. Doctor, I'll need your help. Theodore wants to see me before he dies, and I must be strong."

Dr. Watts was puzzled. "How do you know your brother wants to see you?"

"He came to me in my dreams. He called to me—'I'm tired, Etta,' he told me, 'the end is near. I want to see you. I'll wait.'"

Dr. Watts' brows tightened. "Do you believe in dreams?"

"Of course I do," she said, starting for the door. "That's another advantage that comes with age—you learn to become aware of all your senses. Every sense but common sense," she laughed.

The doctor picked up the black suitcase and followed her into the hall.

"Oh, that reminds me," she said. "In all the excitement of getting here, I forgot to make hotel arrangements."

"I'll have my secretary do that, if you like," he told her, "but I'd better warn you, the only hotel in town isn't much."

"Is it clean?" she asked promptly.

"Oh, yes," he smiled, "it's clean, but it's old."

"Sounds like it's made to order. Old, but clean," she said. She looked up. "I almost stayed at the fanciest motel on the highway."

"What happened?" he asked.

"It didn't work out," she replied. "Now, I think we'd better go."

Dr. Watts followed her down the hall.

The Carmichael Building had been built in the late 1930s. It was a three-story brick structure, housing a fifty-three-bed medical and surgical unit. Etta noticed that it was as spotlessly clean and orderly as the other buildings she had visited.

Dr. Watts led her to the elevator located in the center hall. The self-service lift stopped at the second floor. The left wing of the building was painted pink for the women patients; the right wing walls were decorated in blue enamel. Etta started to comment, "How cute," but decided better.

Dr. Watts took the keys from his pocket and unlocked the door to the men's ward. He led Etta down the corridor to Theodore's room. When Dr. Watts and Etta reached the doorway, a nurse stood up and walked toward them.

"He's sleeping now," she said.

"This is Mr. Morrison's sister, Mrs. Pearson," Dr. Watts told her.

Etta spoke up. "How is he?"

Evading her question, the nurse looked toward the doctor, waiting for his nod before answering.

"It's just a matter of time, Mrs. Pearson," she said. "He's been calling for Etta. Is she family?"

"I'm Etta," the woman answered, walking past her into the room.

The size of the quarters was confining, with barely enough space for the bed and one chair for visitors.

Etta stood for a long while, looking down at her brother. Lying in bed, he appeared so small, almost like a child. His snowy hair curled loosely with perspiration. The oxygen tent billowed slightly as she moved closer.

Dr. Watts touched her arm. "I need to make my rounds, Mrs. Pearson," he said gently. "I'll be in the building if you need me."

She nodded her head.

After the doctor had left, she moved the chair close to the head of the bed. Sitting down, her hand reached out to touch her brother's.

"Theodore, it's me," she said hoarsely. "It's Etta. I'm here, dear. Etta's here."

His eyes opened and searched the room for her face.

"I'm here, Theodore. It's me—Etta. I brought you something, honey."

Her hand groped in her purse, then came back and edged its way under the plastic covering to find his. She placed the object in his palm and closed his fingers around it.

"It's a rock, Theodore. It's a beautiful rock. I thought of you when I found it in my garden. It's streaked with swirling colors of reds and blues, and it's so smooth, just like it's been polished. It's just beautiful.

"Remember how you used to bring rocks to show me? Remember?" she said. "You always told me that the most beautiful rocks came from the creekbed. And I used to tell you to stay away from that creek. But as soon as I'd turn my back, off you'd sneak down there again to search for more rocks. Do you remember, sweetheart? And I'd scold you and you'd promise never to do it again.

"I'll tell you a secret I never told you before," she said, leaning closer. "I always knew you'd go back. I did. I always knew it."

He lay still looking at her. Only his hand moved, feeling the smooth, precious gift she had brought him.

"Oh, Theodore, I loved you so," she sobbed. "I loved you so! You were my favorite—you were. You always knew it!"

Her eyes swelled with tears. "Remember how we used to walk in the evenings and we'd catch fireflies and put them in a jar? Remember how their lights flashed on and off? And we'd pretend they were pirates' treasure? 'They look just like shining gold,' you'd say. You and I always caught more than Agnes and Dot. Dot would get mad and storm back to the house and Agnes would whine and cry and carry on so. Remember, dear? You and me, we never stopped 'til our jars were filled. Then, we'd let them go. Remember how we wondered how many times we had caught the same bugs? Oh, my dear, tell me you remember!"

She pulled her handkerchief from her purse to dry her eyes.

"Remember the day you caught the butterfly and brought it to me in a jar?" she continued. "It was a Painted Lady and so beautiful. And you took it over to Tom Johanson to show him, because you thought it was so much prettier than any he had collected. And remember, Tom showed you how to use the chloroform and mount it on a board?

"And when you came back to the house, you rushed

right past me and ran up the stairs to your room," she said. "I knew something was wrong and I followed you upstairs. When I came into your room, you were crying. 'We killed it!' you said. 'It was so beautiful and we killed it!' And I tried to console you but you kept on crying and saying you had no right to kill it—that you should have turned it loose. And I cried too and told you that we could get rid of it and not think about it anymore. But you said, 'no,' you didn't ever want to forget what you had done. So you put the plaque on your wall to serve as a reminder. I was so proud of you."

Her brother lay watching his visitor in silence. Her large, blue eyes and gentle smile were welcome to him. He saw the young girl's auburn hair pulled back into tight braids. She had not changed. All was the same as it had been so long ago. He closed his eyes and drifted back into sleep.

All day, Etta sat close to Theodore's bed, moving away only when the nurse came to adjust his bedding and check the pressure gauge on the oxygen tank. Dr. Watts stopped in, periodically, to reassure her that he was close by.

In late afternoon, Etta stood by the window watching the orange sun melt into the horizon.

"Etta," she heard her brother's voice call.

"Yes, dear," she replied, remaining where she stood.

His voice was firm and natural. "The rock is beautiful," he said.

Etta didn't move. Instead, she stayed at the window until the sun had escaped the evening sky and darkness had crept across the land. When at last she turned from the window, she didn't look toward the bed, but walked resolutely to the door. Meeting the nurse in the hallway, she told her to call Dr. Watts. She waited there, not returning to her brother's room.

In the corridor, Etta sat on the white wooden bench, her eyes fixed on the blue wall before her. When Dr. Watts came out of Theodore's room, he walked slowly to her . . . to where she waited.

"Mrs. Pearson," he said softly, "are you all right?"

"Yes, Doctor, I'm all right," she answered, looking up. "To tell you the truth, I'm relieved. Forgive me if I'm blunt, but I'm relieved. Why don't you sit down? You must be exhausted."

The doctor sat on the bench beside her. For the length of the corridor, only the two figures broke the monotony of the hollow silence.

"I can't cry," Etta confessed. "I feel no sadness— only finality. Dr. Watts," she said, turning toward him, "I think you and I are much alike. Death is no stranger to us. You have seen it many times in your chosen work, and I have witnessed its touch by simply outliving so many of the ones I've loved. Yes, I think we're very much alike—you and me."

"I feel honored that you think that, Mrs. Pearson," he replied.

"Oh, no, the honor is mine," Etta insisted. "You are a

strong man with useful hands, yet you're not afraid to show kindness. It takes a strong man to give kindness.

"My father was a strong man. My husband was, too, except he drank too much—it's the curse of the bricklayer trade—whiskey with beer chasers—awful stuff! It weakens men. Papa never drank much—a little corn liquor now and then, and hard cider. When my father died," she said, "I thought I would never get over it...and I was right. There's hardly a day goes by that I don't think of him and miss him.

"But Frank...my husband...when he died, I became angry...so angry I could hardly grieve. I didn't understand my feelings then and I'm not sure I do now. I had the strangest feeling that he had deserted me—leaving me to make out the best I could. For the first time in my life, I had to make all of my own decisions. And I resented that. I wasn't prepared.

"My father had made all the decisions at home. And Frank made all the major decisions in our house. Oh, I prepared the meals and sent the children to school, and made the little decisions in the everyday course of events. But the major ones were made by the men. I was raised that way. I'm not sure that was right. It's a terrible thing to do to a woman—to dominate her life so, and then leave her to fend for herself."

"You seem to have done quite well," Dr. Watts said, trying to reassure her.

"I don't think so," she replied. "I closed myself in, making a ritual out of housework and tending my roses. I was afraid to get out and try anything new. When my sister told me I should go to a rest home and live with people my own age, I could have strangled her."

Dr. Watts smiled.

"Don't laugh at me," she said, seriously. "The Bible says our years are numbered. And I believe that. I used to think about my number—wondered how long I had. Well, the number 84 came right into my head one day, and I knew that was it. I believe it. That means I have ten years left. And that frightens me."

"You shouldn't be afraid," Dr. Watts told her.

"It's not the dying that scares me," she explained quickly. "I'm a Baptist and I'm ready for that. It's the living. What am I going to do for ten years? Decisions. Do you see what I mean?"

"I think so."

"Well," she said, "that's something I've got to consider. When I received your telegram, I panicked. I started calling my sisters and my son to see if they would bring me here. Like some child who couldn't think for herself, I didn't believe I could manage on my own. Well, when I found out I had no other choice, I learned I *could* do it myself. Good for me!"

She opened her purse and placed her handkerchief inside. "I spend too much of my time reliving the past. In the last thirty-six hours, I've watched my entire life pass before me like a drowning person is supposed to. That's enough of that!

"Let me tell you something," she said, raising

her index finger. "I'm not going to do that anymore. Why should I go over all of that again? My life wasn't all that interesting the first time around.

"You know," she declared, "it makes me very angry to have taken seventy-four years to discover such a simple thing!"

"Mrs. Pearson," Dr. Watts consoled, "some people never discover it."

"I suppose that's true," she considered. "How very sad." She looked directly at him, "Don't you let yourself make the same mistake.

"Now, there I go again," she said, not waiting for him to reply, "trying to tell everyone else what to do. That's another habit I've got to break."

She paused for a moment. "I'm glad it's over for Theodore. I'm glad I came here."

"So am I," he replied quietly.

"You've been a great deal of help, Dr. Watts," Etta said. "I wish there was something I could do for you."

The doctor smiled. "As a matter of fact, there *is* something you can do for me," he said.

She looked at him questioningly.

"I haven't had dinner and you haven't either. I know a little café in town where the food is unpretentious, but the steaks are thick and the coffee is perked. Would you be my guest for dinner?"

Etta didn't hesitate to answer. "Yes," she said, "I will. I'm a meat and potatoes girl and I drink my coffee black."

"I thought as much," the doctor said, taking her arm.

Together, they walked down the corridor toward the elevator.

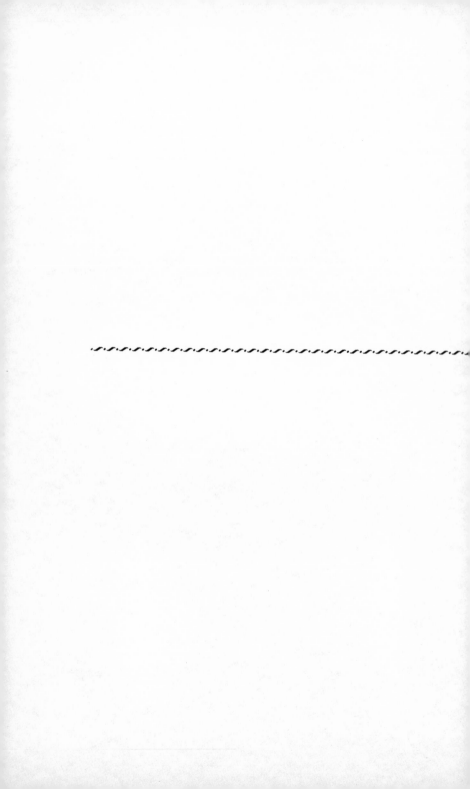

August 16, 1953

Ashes to ashes and dust to dust," the minister said before the open grave. The bronzed casket was lowered into the earth. The workmen removed the straps and pulled them from the shadowed pit. Etta walked across to the mound of dirt piled to the side of the rectangular hole and released the handful of soil, letting it sift over the casket.

Then, she said aloud to the man, "I won't stand for the dirt to be dumped in. It's to be shoveled."

The workmen followed her orders.

She stood there until the grave was filled and the sod had been replaced, concealing the earth's scar.

Dr. Watts took Etta to the station.

"Thank you for everything," she said, standing on the platform. "Remember what I told you—start looking."

"I will," he promised.

Etta turned to board the train, then stopped where she stood. "It doesn't seem right," she said, looking toward the hospital. "This is my last trip to Osawatomie. For nearly forty years, I've been coming here to see Theodore. Now, I have no reason to come back. Forty years—it just doesn't seem right."

She looked back to her friend. "Isn't it strange that after all these years and all those letters, suddenly, it's all over? Do you mind if, once in a while, I write you a note?"

"I'll look forward to it," he answered.

Etta raised her hand and touched his face. "You take good care of yourself—no more sleeping on the couch. You go home at night."

"I will," Dr. Watts replied. He reached into his pocket and pulled out some bills, then handed them to her.

"Oh, I almost forgot," he said. "Your brother earned this money over a period of time, doing odd jobs at the hospital."

Etta looked at the doctor doubtfully. "Are you sure this was Theodore's money?" she asked.

"The staff thought you should have it."

She was bewildered. "Why, there's over fifty dollars here. What should I do with it?"

"Spend it on yourself!" he ordered. "Do something with it you've never done before."

As the train pulled away from the station, Etta waved to her friend. Then she looked down at the folded money she held in her hand. Once more, she questioned if she should have taken it. And now that she had it, what should she do with it?

"Spend it on yourself," she repeated aloud. "Do something you've never done before."

12

"Well, there's no use just sitting here on her porch!" Dorothy fumed as she strolled back and forth impatiently. "We have no idea when she'll be back."

"Let's wait a little longer, Dot," Agnes whined. "Harry and I have to drive back to Amarillo in the morning and I would like to see Etta before I leave."

Dorothy paced back across the porch. "The neighbors probably think we're crazy as loons just sitting around here like this."

The group ignored Dorothy's remark as they had her other comments during most of the afternoon. Agnes said little. She had sat in the rocker, restlessly moving back and forth. Alfred and Harry passed the time reading the Sunday paper. Other than answering "uh-huh" or "huh-uh" to questions posed directly to them, they had kept quiet.

Robert and Jessie had arrived later in the afternoon to join them in their vigil. Robert smoked one cigarette after the other and flipped the shortened butts across the sidewalk. Other than, "Hello," and "I'm fine," Jessie hadn't offered a word. It was evident that she and Robert were not on the friendliest of terms.

But Dorothy hadn't been quiet for a moment. Ordering everyone about—sending Marjorie inside to make lemonade, shooing the men off to meet all the trains arriving from Joplin and Kansas City—she remained in perpetual motion and emotion.

"Well, there are only two more trains this evening," she preached on. "If Etta's not on one of those, I won't know what to think!"

"Maybe," Agnes said, nervously, "she decided to catch a bus in Joplin."

"How are we supposed to know?" Dorothy stormed. "I don't understand Etta at all, not telling us what her plans are!"

"Well, Dot," Agnes commented, "she did send us a telegram yesterday."

"That's what I mean!" Dorothy petulantly stamped her foot. "What kind of message was that to send at a time like this? 'Now you can buy flowers,' it said. Information! What kind of information is that?"

Marjorie had considered the message complete but she said nothing.

"Here we sit," Dorothy grumbled. "Poor Theodore is dead. If we hadn't called the hospital long distance

today, we wouldn't have known that the funeral
was this morning, and that Etta had already left.
Looks like she would have called to tell us when she'd
be in. It's just like her—keeping us guessing!"

Agnes changed her position in the rocker. "I bet
she'll be on that seven-thirty train."

"That's four hours," Dorothy fussed, "four hours to
wait on this hot porch!"

"We could go inside," Agnes suggested.

"It's just as hot in there," Dorothy snapped. "No,
we'll wait out here. Looks like the least she could have
done is to let us know!"

A yellow cab turned the corner and pulled into
the driveway. The driver took a black suitcase from
the front seat. Dorothy stood stiffly by the banister
as Agnes craned her neck to see the taxi. Harry
and Alfred looked up from their papers. Robert stepped
down from the porch as the driver opened the back
door to assist his passenger out. Etta looked up to
see the members of the reception committee. She paid
the driver, took her suitcase, and started up the walk.

"Here, Mother," Robert offered, running out to meet
her, "I'll take your suitcase."

"No thank you," she said, walking by him and
climbing the steps to the porch.

"Etta, why didn't you let us know what train
you were arriving on?" Dorothy protested. "We didn't
expect you until seven-thirty."

Agnes cleared her throat. "Hello, Etta. Harry and I
were afraid we wouldn't get to see you. We'll have
to drive home in the morning."

"Have a safe trip," Etta replied.

"When did your train get in?" Dorothy asked.

"I didn't come on the train," she told them flatly.

"Well, how then?" Dorothy questioned.

"I flew," Etta announced, "on a DC 3, from Joplin."

"My word!" Agnes gasped.

"It was thrilling," Etta said, walking past her waiting relatives. She opened the screen door, carried her suitcase straight to the bedroom, and set it on the floor by the dresser. She couldn't reach the bed soon enough to satisfy her. She had sorely missed the feel of her own bed while she was away. She sat on the edge, untied her shoes and pulled them off her tired feet.

Her bed seemed to respond to her body and she rested her head against the comfort of her pillow. Closing her eyes, Etta attempted to release all thoughts from her mind.

"Aunt Etta," Marjorie said, meekly, as she entered the room.

"Yes, Marjorie?" Etta answered slowly.

"The others are waiting for you on the porch."

"Are they now?" she replied dully.

Marjorie walked around the bed, pausing momentarily to look at the snow-white hair framing her aunt's round face. Gently, the girl sat down on the side of the bed.

"Aunt Etta," she said, "I want you to know I'm sorry I didn't go with you."

Etta didn't open her eyes. "That's all right, child."

"I just couldn't, Aunt Etta," Marjorie tried to explain. "I guess sixteen doesn't mean I've grown up after all. You see, I was afraid. I have never been close to death before and I was afraid."

Etta's eyes opened with understanding. Her hand reached out to the young girl beside her. "Death isn't to be feared, child. It's as natural as living. It's like the darkened room beyond a closed door. We may hesitate to open that door only because we're uncertain of what waits on the other side. But, once the door is open and the blinds are raised, sunshine fills every corner, and we find our own room waiting for us. It's the opening of the door we fear, Marjorie, not the room."

"Oh, Aunt Etta, forgive me!"

"There's nothing to forgive, dear," Etta told the girl. "Your place in my heart will never change, for you found your way there long ago. I'm only sorry you weren't with me to see your Uncle Theodore, for truly he was prepared to open that final door."

"Aunt Etta, did he know you were there?" Marjorie asked. "Did he really know?"

Etta's eyes deepened. "He knew," she replied. "For one fleeting moment, he knew."

Marjorie stood up. "The others—what shall I tell the others?" she asked.

"Tell them to go home," Etta replied.

"No . . . wait . . . I'll do it myself."

Acknowledgments

My sincere thanks to Dorothy Bishop who, at the time I began writing *Theodore*, was Director of Public Information at Osawatomie State Hospital, Osawatomie, Kansas. Mrs. Bishop kindly arranged for me to tour the facilities where Mr. Morrison had lived, and allowed me to interview both staff members and patients who had known him. I am indebted to her for supplying needed information from Mr. Morrison's medical records, and copies of Etta Pearson's correspondence. Some of those letters are excerpted within this book.

I appreciate the assistance offered by J. Russell Mills, the present Superintendent of Osawatomie State Hospital. He provided pertinent materials which helped validate the historical accuracy of events, places and people.

I also wish to thank my wife, Nancy, for her extraordinary help in preparing the typed manuscripts. I doubt that any book has ever been assembled with more love and care.

I am indebted to my daughter, Teresa, for her help in reading and editing the early stages of the manuscript.

I am grateful to Margaret Baldwin for her thoughtful and sensitive editing of the completed manuscript, and to Jack Ferguson for seeing the potential of the book.

And to my grandmother, Mary Etta Pearson, I thank her for living her life with such grit and determination, and for being the person she was. I only wish she could have lived to see the book in print.

And to Theodore Morrison, my granduncle, who lived so much of his life in anonymity and confinement — may this writing serve as a testimony that his years were not spent unnoticed.